THE BARKS & BEANS CAFE
MYSTERY SERIES

COLD DRIP

THE BARKS & BEANS CAFE MYSTERY SERIES:
BOOK 6

HEATHER DAY GILBERT

Cold Drip

Cover Design by Elizabeth Mackey of Elizabeth Mackey Graphics

Published by WoodHaven Press

Series: Gilbert, Heather Day. Barks & Beans Cafe Mystery; 6

Subject: Detective and Mystery Stories; Coffeehouses—Fiction; Dogs—Fiction Genre: Mystery Fiction

Author Information & Newsletter: **http://www.heatherdaygilbert.com**

FROM THE BACK COVER

Welcome to the Barks & Beans Cafe, a quaint place where folks pet shelter dogs while enjoying a cup of java...and where murder sometimes pays a visit.

Thanksgiving is on the way, and Macy's thrilled when her boyfriend Titan says he's coming to town for a week-long visit. She plans to take him to some of her favorite haunts, including the sprawling caverns nearby.

But when the lights go out during their underground tour and a local society darling plunges to her death, Macy can't shake the feeling that the cave's slippery floors weren't entirely to blame. She taps into the admittedly limited skills of her upscale barista, Milo, to do a little snooping in the moneyed circles he moves in. When he unearths a sink-hole of lies, Macy slides straight toward a killer who's not about to stop until every leak is sealed...permanently.

Join siblings Macy and Bo Hatfield as they sniff out crimes in their hometown...with plenty of dogs along for the ride! The Barks & Beans Cafe cozy mystery series features a small town, an amateur sleuth, and no swearing or graphic scenes. Find all the books at heatherdaygilbert.com!

The Barks & Beans Cafe series in order:

- Book 1: No Filter
- Book 2: Iced Over
- Book 3: Fair Trade
- Book 4: Spilled Milk
- Book 5: Trouble Brewing
- Book 6: Cold Drip
- Book 7: Roast Date

1

I cradled my second cup of French press coffee, savoring our Barks & Beans Cafe house blend as I stood on my porch. My beat-up plaid coat didn't quite cut the chill of the snowy November day. But I'd planned to enjoy my Friday off in spite of the weather, so I was spending a slow morning lounging around with my Great Dane, Coal. As he chased his favorite ball in the back garden, my phone buzzed.

My boyfriend Titan's deep voice made me smile. "Hey there. Just wanted to let you know I'm taking the entire week of Thanksgiving off, so I've booked a cabin in the woods just outside town. I'll come in on Monday. I figured I might as well make a holiday of it, since I was driving up for Thanksgiving dinner anyway. I hope that sounds all right?"

"Are you kidding me? That's fantastic!" Coal loped up the porch steps, picking up on my excitement. His perpetually pricked ears angled my way, as if he wanted to figure out what I was saying. "I'll figure out some fun things to do while you're in. There's a reason Lewisburg was voted America's 'Coolest Small Town,' you know."

He chuckled. "It'll always be America's coolest town as long as you're in it."

"Thanks. I do love this place." I glanced around my back yard, rubbing behind Coal's ears. My great-aunt Athaleen's well-established flowerbeds had died, but I knew where each patch of iris, tulips, and beebalm bumped up against the rosebushes lining the boxwood hedges. I appreciated every inch of the three-story Colonial house I'd grown up in, even though my brother Bo had since renovated the front half into our cafe. I planned to stay in Lewisburg for the rest of my life, but I hadn't yet verbalized that intention to Titan. His family came from the northern part of the state, and, although he currently lived in rural Virginia, I wasn't sure where he ultimately wanted to settle down.

We'd have to talk about future plans someday, but, in true youngest child fashion, I preferred to live in the *now* and let reality slap me in the face later.

After telling Titan goodbye, I headed inside to refresh my coffee and see if I had any Thanksgiving decor items I could set out. Coal followed me in and, as usual, drank a copious amount of water before settling down on his pillow in the living room. He watched with an amused look as I dragged out a couple of boxes of knickknacks, placed a wilted-looking wreath on the door, and situated a faded cornucopia on the table. I did find three autumn-scented candles, which I positioned on the kitchen counter, next to some small pumpkins I'd picked up at Halloween. Since Bo and I had invited two other guests to celebrate Thanksgiving at my house—my neighbor Vera and Bo's girlfriend Summer—I wanted to get things looking fallish.

After my low-key effort to dress up the house, I decided to take an early lunch break and grab one of Charity's sandwiches at the cafe. Our cherubic-faced baker was always coming up with gourmet concoctions, which I never failed to enjoy—perhaps to the detriment of my figure. Although I thought of myself as "pleasantly plump," like Bess in the Nancy Drew mysteries, Titan had once bashfully told me I looked like a Greek goddess, so I'd decided not to feel guilty for eating the foods that made my life brighter.

I headed down the sidewalk that ran alongside our corner lot, using the cafe's front door instead of the interior door that connected with my half of the house. I didn't like customers peering into my private space.

Milo, our twenty-something barista, gave me a grin and a nod as I entered. He was working the coffee section with Bo. Milo hadn't been wearing his fashion glasses lately, so his unusual blue-gray eyes now took center stage, along with his unruly dark blond hair. He brought a lot of class—and a lot of *sass*—to the cafe, and he kept all our social media up-to-date. We still weren't sure why he'd chosen to work for us, given the upper-class family he came from, but he'd become our most efficient barista, and the customers—especially the female ones —loved him.

Bo walked over to give me a hug. His red hair was getting a bit long on top, but I knew he'd get it cut soon. He'd never liked it when his rogue curls grew out. Given his bulging muscles and his confident demeanor, Bo effortlessly attracted even more attention than Milo. But now that he'd asked Summer to be his girlfriend, I knew he'd never look at another woman. My brother's loyalty ran even deeper than mine, which was saying something. In fact, I'd had to *un*learn loyalty when my husband Jake had demanded a divorce a few years ago.

"Everything going well?" he asked.

I nodded. "Titan's coming in on Monday and staying the week, actually. He's got a cabin about thirty minutes from here, so he'll be able to do some touristy things this visit."

"You should go to the caves," Bo said. "Remember how much we used to love those?"

A memory intruded into my thoughts of me following Auntie A along damp cavern floors with my flat-soled Dollar Store tennis shoes. I'd started slipping toward a steep drop, but Bo had grabbed my elbow and held fast until I'd regained my footing. "I don't know if I was the one who loved the caves." I frowned.

As if picking up on the direction of my thoughts, he said, "I wouldn't have let you fall."

"I know. But I'm not sure if I'm ready to go back. I'll think about it."

While he headed back to the coffee bar, I walked toward the doggie section, where Bristol, our college-bound barista, was talking to a smaller, brindled-looking black dog. She held out her open palm, and, to my surprise, the dog stretched a paw up to give her a high five.

"Isn't this doggie smart?" she asked. "Her name is Sadie. She's a little older—her owner had to move to a smaller place that didn't allow dogs. They said she's a mix of Blue Heeler and Boston Terrier. She honestly seems to understand everything I'm saying."

I walked closer, and the dog's compassionate brown eyes met my own. She almost seemed to smile at me. I caught my breath. "She really is intelligent. She reminds me of a dog I had in high school that I considered one of my best friends."

"I hope she'll get adopted right away," Bristol said. "Even though she's getting up in years, she could be a great companion to someone."

The cafe door opened with a flourish, and a posse of young women strutted in. Like a gaggle of geese, they formed a loose formation around the person who was clearly their leader—a tall, tan blonde whose flipped hair was reminiscent of Farrah Fawcett's.

The leader stalked directly to the counter. From the indifferent look on Milo's face, I suspected he knew these women and wasn't impressed.

Bristol had left off her interactions with Sadie and, like me, was watching the scenario playing out in the Beans section of the cafe.

The tall woman rapped at the counter with her noticeably long nails. "Milo, would you be a dear and make me a grande iced sugar-free vanilla latte with soymilk?" She paused, adjusting the chain strap of her black Chanel purse. "I can say it slower if you like."

Although I couldn't see the smug look on her face, I could hear it in her tone. I didn't want customers thinking they could treat my baristas disdainfully, but I wasn't sure how to deter her. Bo, who was standing at the espresso maker, shot her a look that said everything I was thinking. I hoped she backed off. What kind of beef did she have with Milo?

Bristol, who had been Milo's unspoken love interest for several months, stood to her feet. I knew she wanted to give that girl a what-for, as Auntie A would say, but we couldn't very well go ganging up on the customers. I gestured to her chair, hoping she'd sit down again. "It'll be okay. Bo's got it under control," I whispered.

As the woman made her way to the other end of the counter, her friends filed up to place their orders. Milo seemed completely unfazed by their leader's impertinence —at least until she raised her voice and practically shouted, "You hard-up for cash, Milo? I thought your daddy was doing pretty well. Of course, I know your mom doesn't work."

A wicked little grin spread across Milo's face. Without missing a beat, he responded, "And what does your stepmom do again, Darby? Some kind of side hustle, isn't it?"

This brought the aforementioned Darby up short, and she fell silent. A redhead who'd been second in line strode over to her friend's side, giving her back a light, encouraging pat. The third in line, a brunette, tossed her mane as Milo took her order, but he seemed as unconcerned as a CEO observing his underlings cutting up in the break room. I had to admire this new side of Milo. He had a certain unstudied air of command about him. I rarely saw it, since Bo was the ultimate leader in our cafe, but I made a mental note that Milo could definitely hold his own.

Once the girl gang had settled in at a long table in the back corner, I walked over to Milo. "You okay?" I asked quietly. "Is she some kind of frenemy?"

"You could say that." He stacked clean coffee mugs on the counter. "We move in the same circles, but Darby Whitmore can't stand for anyone to show her up—including her own friends. Each of the girls in that group knows she's disposable, and if she gets too popular in comparison with Darby, she's out."

"That's awful," I said. "What did you do to attract her wrath?"

He shrugged. "My dad's richer than her dad was. Victor Whitmore owned a lot of gas and oil rights in Pennsylvania, and when he died in his fifties of a stroke, Darby inherited his fortune. She's irritated that she's not the top dog right now. Plus, she recently split with her boyfriend, so that makes her extra unpleasant."

Just as I was about to ask Milo for more details, Darby's redheaded friend walked over. I scurried back to the Barks section, knowing Bristol would want the full report on who Darby was. Glancing back, I saw that the redhead seemed to be speaking kindly to Milo, even laughing at one point. Maybe Darby hadn't managed to kill all the civility amongst her crew, but I found myself hoping they wouldn't return to the Barks & Beans Cafe anytime soon.

2

The weekend flew by, and before I knew it, Monday had arrived. Since I was taking the afternoon off to hang out with Titan before he settled in his cabin, I finished my morning shift before heading to a sandwich shop to meet up with him.

After situating myself at a table that faced the door, I was rewarded with a prime view of the tall drink of water that was my boyfriend when he walked in. Titan McCoy—whose last name provided no end of jokes for us Hatfield siblings—was not the kind of man to be ignored. He was six foot five, and while I should've felt like a shrimp standing next to him at a mere five foot three, instead I felt some indescribable sense of comfort.

He'd let his thick brown curls grow out a little since we'd first met last year, and they perfectly framed his golden brown eyes. When he saw me, he gave me the kind of full-on smile that seemed like a gift. Given his line of work as an FBI agent, he usually wore a poker face.

"Am I late?" He took long strides toward me. "I hope you went ahead and ordered."

"You're not late. For once, I'm early. And yes, I ordered my sandwich and a sweet tea for both of us. You'll want to order your food."

"Sounds great."

After our sandwiches arrived—a Rueben for him and a turkey on rye for me—I asked for an update on crime lord Leo Moreau, a man who'd run drugs, stolen artwork, and even trafficked humans through our state until he'd been recently collared for his deeds. He especially hated my brother Bo, who was the DEA agent—now thankfully retired—who'd put the final nail in Leo's coffin and sent him to prison.

Leo's own wife, Anne Louise, was the one who'd called Bo and handed him that nail on a silver platter. Although it was clear she wanted to get Leo out of her life, her ultimate intentions were far more murky. Did she just want solitude to enjoy the wealth her husband had amassed? Or was she planning to take over the reins of Leo's dark empire, activating the network of loyal henchmen she'd stolen from him?

"Leo's been fairly quiet in prison." Titan took a sip of his tea, setting the ice rattling in the glass. "He seems to be keeping a low profile."

"What about Anne Louise—is she making any moves to take over?"

"That's why I'm meeting up with a friend from the Bureau while I'm in. Julius Vos is an art expert who keeps his finger on the pulse of high-profile artwork that goes missing or that shows up on the black market. We are aware that Anne Louise has a fondness for acquiring and selling jewels and art, and, unfortunately, there's been an uptick in that kind of activity since Leo was imprisoned."

"I suppose shuttling jewels and artwork to the black market isn't as bad as the human trafficking and drug running her husband had gotten into," I mused.

One side of his lips quirked downward. "That's what you'd think, but it depends on what she does with all the money she's accumulating. When someone's willing to stoop to crime to get what they want—even crime that isn't as violent—it's a slippery slope."

I sighed, irritated that the Moreaus were like the gift that kept on giving. "Moving on to less villainous topics...Bo suggested we visit the local caverns today, since you haven't seen them yet. Would that be something you'd like to do?"

"Sure." Titan extended a long arm across the table, opening his hand with a hopeful look. I placed my hand in his large palm, and he closed his fingers around it. Holding hands with Titan was the kind of grounding experience that always made me breathe a little deeper and see the world in brighter colors.

Even though I'd avoided the caverns for years, I knew that Titan, like Bo, would keep me safe if anything went amiss, which was unlikely, given the fact that people safely toured there all the time. Plus, I was a grown woman, capable of watching my own footing. Just because I'd had a bad experience with caves as a child didn't mean I'd have one again. That drop had probably seemed a lot steeper in my six-year-old mind than it actually was.

THE CAVERNS HAD a jam-packed gift shop that enticed me with a wide variety of polished gemstones, hand-crafted jewelry, and sweatshirts. Titan wandered over to examine a dinosaur reproduction in a glass case, so I took the opportunity to pick out a heather gray hoodie in his size. I hoped this place would become a warm memory for him—and for me.

As the cashier rang me up, he explained that the tour was self-guided, so we'd just need to follow the clearly marked walkways to make a loop through the caverns. I asked him to keep my bag behind the counter until we returned from the tour.

I was about to head toward Titan when three women came in, cutting me off as they strode directly toward the checkout counter. I recognized Darby Whitmore immediately, along with the redhead and the brunette who'd come with her to the cafe. What a weird coincidence.

Darby murmured something to the cashier, who looked to be about her age, and he gave a nervous laugh. He seemed to be dazzled by his upscale customer.

I tried not to stare at Darby's outfit. If she was planning to tour the caves, her black satin shorts and sleeveless blouse would certainly be too lightweight for the cool, rock-lined world below. She had thought to tie a cropped fuchsia jacket around her waist, so at least she'd have an extra layer —insufficient as it was. Her ballet flats probably had even flimsier tread than my tennis shoes had, all those years ago. Maybe she wasn't doing the tour at all.

She caught me looking at her and gave me a presumptuous smile, as if acknowledging she was the center of attention. "Weren't you at that dog cafe we visited?" she asked, as if I were some underling who happened to work there.

"Yes, my brother and I own the cafe." I shouldn't need to clarify my position to her, but something deep inside forced me to.

As my social standing went up, she seemed to warm to me. "Nice to meet you." She gestured to the brunette at her side, who gave me an apathetic glance. "This is my friend Olivia Randolph—her father runs the medical center in town." As she pointed to the redhead, who had the type of long, curly hair you'd see in a shampoo commercial, she tossed out, "And this is Florence Bailey. She's been my friend since kindergarten."

Florence, who seemed the most unpretentious of the three, smiled and said a polite hello. I noticed Darby hadn't mentioned what her father did.

"Are you all taking the tour?" I asked.

To my surprise, Darby said, "We are. The salt cave spa is our favorite place, so we figured we'd check out these caves, too."

I didn't have the heart to tell her this wasn't a small cave like the spa, where you sat in comfy chairs, listened to relaxing music, and basked in the subtle glow of numerous pink salt lamps, but I guessed she'd figure it out soon enough.

As the swanky trio headed for the entry door to the caves, I walked over to Titan, who was examining a pair of deep green geode bookends.

"Would you like these?" he asked. "I know you have a lot of books, and these looked like something you might like."

As a matter of fact, green shades were my favorites,

since my May birthstone was an emerald. I grinned and gave him a side-hug. "I love them."

Although I was sure they were heavy, he picked them up like they were snack bags of popcorn and carried them over to the checkout counter. After paying for them, he asked the cashier, "Could you keep these here until we come out?"

The young man gave a brief nod and placed the bag behind the counter, alongside my bag with the sweatshirt.

"Are you ready to go?" Titan asked me.

I looped my arm into the crook of his. "Definitely."

THE WALKWAY WAS ANGLED at a pretty serious slant as we descended below ground level. Above us, the concrete ceilings were vaulted, giving the impression this place would make a great bunker if the need ever arose.

We could hear Darby and her friends talking ahead of us, but we took our time examining the unusual stalactite and stalagmite formations along the sides.

"I always forget which is which," Titan said.

"Stalactites are tight to the ceiling—that's how I remember it." I took a photo of a frothy looking stalactite that tumbled from the cave's ceiling like a waterfall.

Although the lighting was a little more dim than I'd like, it was easy to follow the paved pathway. Sturdy wooden handrails lined the edge—a smart new addition since I'd toured as a child. I was feeling quite safe and enjoying the earthy, cool smells of being underground when all the lights went out.

I stood stock-still, my grip on the handrail tightening.

Titan said, "You okay?" He stepped back to wrap a muscled forearm around my waist.

"I'm good," I lied, trying to control my breathing. "Let me turn on my phone light."

A woman screamed in front of us, and terror clutched at me. The group of friends had been nearing a steeper area when the lights went out, just past some stairs in front of us.

Titan clicked on his phone light. Together, we aimed our lights into the distance, but in the pitch black of the caverns, the circle from their beams didn't reach beyond the top of the steps. "Is everything all right up there?" he shouted.

Instead of a calm reassurance, another woman's scream pierced the darkness.

Titan didn't waste time. "Can you stay here?" he asked. "I'll go on ahead."

I was only too happy to stay put. "Of course. I'll keep my light on."

I shone the beam on Titan until he'd made his way up two sets of steps. Once he reached the top, he stepped out of my view.

It seemed to take forever, but the lights finally came back on. I was at a loss to understand why they'd gone out in the first place.

I clung to the stair railings as I moved forward, taking my time in case the lights cut out again. Once I topped the little hill, I tried to make sense of the scene in front of me.

Florence and Titan stood on a wooden platform that overlooked a flat rock formation on the right. Just beyond the flat area, there was a steep dropoff into a darkened hole. Florence's mascara was smeared where tears had streaked down her face. She was sobbing something about Darby, but I couldn't understand her.

Meanwhile, Olivia, who had been standing some distance beyond Florence, was heading back toward us.

I hurried closer to Titan and Florence. I didn't want to ask what had happened, because my gut was telling me it was something horrible.

As Olivia reached her incoherent friend and wrapped an arm around her, Titan answered my unasked question. "She said Darby must've fallen over that ledge."

I was dumbfounded. "But how? It's way out past those flat rocks."

He turned his phone light on again and, to my horror, climbed under the railing and onto the flat rock area.

"What are you *doing*?" I asked.

"I need to look for her." Watching his footing, he carefully edged forward. I didn't want to think of him reaching the ledge that gave onto the hole.

"This isn't safe! You need a rope or something. If she fell off, so could you!" My voice was shaky.

He glanced back at me. "Someone needs to go up to the gift shop and let them know what happened so they can call emergency services. I haven't checked to see if we have cell service down here, but I doubt it."

I threw a desperate look toward Olivia and asked, "Could you do that?" I was unwilling to leave Titan alone on his self-imposed mission, and Florence was in no shape to go anywhere. "I'll stay with her," I added.

"Okay." Olivia made her way toward a side loop where

our trail merged with the return path, I supposed so people could cut the tour short if they wanted.

I placed a steadying hand on Florence's arm. When her gasping sobs started to slow, I asked, "Can you tell me what happened?"

"Darby was ahead of me," she said. "She slipped on a wet spot on the step, but she just laughed it off and said she should've worn better shoes. When we reached this platform, she decided to get a photo near the flat rocks. She liked that stalagmite on the edge." She motioned toward a tall stalagmite that resembled an ice cream cone, rising up from the rock wall. Taking a deep breath, she said, "She started climbing under the railing to get a selfie on the flat area. I told her not to, but it was too late, because the lights went off."

A fresh burst of tears overtook her. "I heard her gasp, and then I heard two terrible noises. Her phone must've clattered onto rocks at the bottom of that hole, and then..." She swiped at her eyes. "And then, I heard this thud. I couldn't get my phone light on because my battery's dead."

I glanced toward Titan. To my relief, he hadn't walked all the way to the ledge. Instead, he was standing a few paces back, holding his phone light aloft and trying to light the cavern below.

"Can you see anything?" I asked.

He shook his head, his gaze fixed on the cavern. "There's no way I'd be able to see her from up here. We need more lights and a rope crew."

Florence shivered. "Do you think it's a steep enough drop to..." Her voice trailed off.

Trying not to jump to the worst-case scenario, I said, "Maybe she just got knocked out or broke a bone."

"But either way, she should be calling out to us by now, right?"

Titan and I exchanged glances. That was what was worrying me—we hadn't heard a peep from the gaping hole below.

3

Voices and shouts sounded as a small group headed our way. Olivia was leading the charge, carrying a flashlight, and the cashier trailed behind her. A couple in their mid-fifties brought up the rear, wearing concerned looks. I had to assume they'd been in the gift shop and had offered to help.

As the cashier approached the railing, Titan quickly explained that no one was to join him on the other side because it was too slippery. No one asked why *he* was allowed to stand on that side of the railing, but that's because Titan wore his air of authority like a second skin.

"I've called Darby's stepmom, Nina. She's on her way," Olivia offered.

"Thank you." Titan turned to the cashier. "Did you call emergency services or the police?"

"I did." The young man seemed anxious, but that was understandable, given the fact that he'd basically lost someone on his watch.

"Why did the lights go out?" Titan demanded. "I take it that's not a normal part of the tour?"

"Definitely not," the guy said. "I think it must've shorted out or something. I don't know much about wiring, but we've never had issues like that before. And I didn't even know the lights were out, so they must've come back on by themselves."

"Could I use that flashlight?" Titan asked Olivia.

She nodded and handed it over. As Titan took a step closer to the chasm, I held my breath. When he extended one of his long arms, the light's powerful beams actually seemed to penetrate the darkness.

Suddenly, Titan said, "I see something...it's bright pink." He called out, "Darby! Darby, can you hear me?"

Florence sucked in her breath. "That must be Darby's jacket. It's fuchsia. It was tied around her waist when she went under the railing."

The older woman piped up. "Oh, dear. She must've fallen for sure."

I shot her a hush-this-instant look, and she fell silent. The last thing Florence needed was someone blurting out that her friend must be dead.

Titan turned to the cashier. "How steep is this drop, do you know?"

The guy shook his head. "No, but I think the owner is on his way—he'll be able to tell you."

Three men in hiking boots and long-sleeved black T-shirts emblazoned with a yellow "SAR" on the front showed up, along with a couple of officers from the sheriff's department. After introducing themselves as the search and rescue team and getting a brief rundown of the situation, they headed under the railing to set up their equipment.

Titan came over to me and spoke quietly. "I think I'll stick around and help them awhile. I've had some training in this area, and I figure they can use all the help they can get."

Before I could respond, an older man with dark, messy hair came hurrying toward us. He extended a hand toward one of the officers. "I'm Keith Rogers—I own the caverns. What happened?"

After the officer gave a quick explanation, one of the search team members looked up from the rope harness he was stepping into. "What's the depth on this hole, sir?"

Keith's answer was quick. "That's the one we call the bottomless pit. It's around fifty feet down."

Titan's face blanched a bit, so I knew it was the kind of drop Darby probably couldn't have survived.

Olivia glanced at her phone. "I know this is terrible timing, but I need to get back for an online call with a client. I'm a holistic eating coach, and they count on these sessions to stay on track." She asked the deputy, "Is it okay if I leave? I can give you my number."

"Actually, it would be best if everyone left, except Search and Rescue and the deputies," the officer answered. "Let me take your names and numbers first, in case we have any questions."

One by one, bystanders began to file out of the cave. Florence lingered behind, giving a whimper as one of the rescue team members was lowered over the edge.

I placed a firm hand under Florence's elbow. "Why don't I take you home," I suggested, knowing she shouldn't be driving right now.

"We came in Darby's car," she murmured. "I can't just leave it here."

"It'll be okay," Titan said firmly. "I'll let her stepmother know about it when she gets here."

As we turned to leave, I heard Titan asking Keith if he was right in thinking he'd heard a stream running through the bottom of the chasm.

"There sure is. It's sure to be swollen up now, due to all that melted snow."

One of the SAR team members asked, "Where does the stream let out?"

Keith made a sweeping gesture. "It dumps into a creek that gives into the Greenbrier River, eventually."

Like me, the SAR team was probably contemplating the possibility that even if Darby had survived the fall, she might have landed in the stream.

Florence trudged behind me up the steep tunnel incline. At the top, we exited the caverns and stepped into the gift shop. The cashier had returned to his post, and he looked even more on-edge than before. For the first time, I noticed he was wearing a small nametag that said *Gabe*. "What's going on down there?" he asked. "Have they found her?"

"They're just lowering down now." Glancing toward the counter, I asked, "Did you have our two bags? The sweatshirt and the geode bookends? I'll pick those up now, if you don't mind."

"Of course." Gabe pulled both bags from behind the counter as Florence stood in the middle of the shop, her gaze fixed on nothing in particular. The moment I had our purchases in hand, I steered her out the door, which now bore a *Closed* sign. In the gentle fall sunlight, I pointed toward my car and walked her that way.

She shared her address so I could plug it into my

phone, but not much else. I could understand why she had no interest in making conversation. After all, she'd watched her closest friend approach the edge of a precipice, then, when the cave lights went out, she'd heard her tumble onto the rocks fifty feet below. The rocks and stalagmites in the caverns jutted up at random angles, so I hated to think what Darby might have landed on.

As we drove the quiet streets in town, it occurred to me that Olivia wasn't nearly as ripped up about Darby's possible demise as Florence was. She'd bailed out to take a conference call. If one of my closest friends had fallen into a cavern, I definitely would've canceled any business and stuck around as long as they'd let me.

"Are you and Olivia close?" I asked, trying to understand the dynamics of Darby's friend group.

Florence nodded, but there was a moment's hesitation before she answered. "Sure. Darby and I have been friends the longest, but Olivia and the others joined our group over the past few years." Her hazel eyes met mine. "I know Olivia can come across as a little rude, but she really has a heart of gold."

Olivia hadn't seemed nearly as rude as Darby, but I decided not to point that out. We'd reached Florence's house, which turned out to be a modest one-story just outside Lewisburg. I'd expected her to live in one of the swanky areas of town, like on Rhododendron Drive.

Florence still looked shell-shocked, so I offered to walk her in, but she refused. In a last-ditch effort to keep her steady, I said, "You might want to drop into our cafe sometime so you can pet the shelter dogs. It's kind of like therapy. I'll make sure you get a free coffee, on the house."

She finally smiled. "That's very sweet. I love dogs and

coffee, so I might just take you up on that." She gave a forlorn wave and walked up her driveway.

As I backed out, I got a call from Titan, so I put it on speakerphone.

"We didn't find Darby," he said. "We considered lowering a scent dog, but that would be a pointless effort. We've examined all the rocky area, and the only other place she could be is in the stream. I just don't understand it—the rocks would've proved deadly in a fall, so it makes no sense her body's not down here. She must've somehow rolled into the stream and gotten swept away, so we'll have to move the search outdoors." He took a deep breath. "We did find her phone, and the screen was cracked. We couldn't get the device unlocked, so the police tech department is working on it. Not that it will shed any light on things, unless she happened to be taking a video before the cave went dark."

"Do you need me to pick you up now? I'm on the road anyway."

"Sure—if you don't mind. Have you told Bo yet?"

"No, but I was planning on dropping by the cafe to let him know. I'm especially concerned about my barista Milo, since he runs in Darby's circles. I'm not sure how he'll take the news, even though they didn't seem fond of each other."

"That'll work. I'll grab a coffee while you're filling them in."

Trying to encourage Titan, I said, "Kylie's working this afternoon, and she makes the best Irish cream lattes. I know those are your favorite."

"I can almost taste it now. Thanks for the heads-up."

Once Titan had gotten situated at a table with his latte, I took Bo and Milo aside in the back room and told them about what had happened to Darby. Milo's face registered a level of shock I didn't realize he could feel, given his habitually nonchalant manner.

"That's insane," he breathed, his voice cracking. "That's impossible. Why did the lights go out?"

"We don't know yet, but I'm sure the police are looking into it," I said.

He pulled his phone from his pocket and flipped through a feed, then turned the screen for us to see. "Look at this photo she posted. It must've been just before she fell." His voice was incredulous.

Sure enough, in the photo, Darby was standing on the wet, flat rocks outside the railing. She'd pursed her lips and jutted her hips to the side, as if striking a modeling pose. Her fuchsia jacket, which had later dropped into the pit with her, was still tied around her waist.

What a foolish way to go. Breaking the rules for the perfect selfie. I knew it wasn't the first time someone had fallen to her death trying to look impressive on social media, but it was no less tragic.

"But if she died in the fall, where is she?" Bo asked the obvious question.

"Titan said they're guessing she must've somehow bounced when she hit the ground and wound up in the underground stream, which was overflowing due to melted snow. It gives out onto a creek, then the Greenbrier."

"Does the search team need help?" Bo had been born the vigilant protector type, and he never hesitated to jump in and get his hands dirty. I was certain those qualities had made him an outstanding Marine and DEA agent.

"You could ask Titan." I threw another glance at the visibly shaken Milo. "You want me to fill in for you today?" I offered. "Maybe you should go meet up with some of your friends and talk about this."

He shook his head. "It's better for me to stick around. Work will distract me a little."

As Milo headed back to the coffee bar, Bo said, "Am I still doing supper tonight? I've invited Summer, but if you don't feel like hanging out, I can just send food over for you and Titan. I was just making lemon butter chicken in the slow cooker."

"No, we'll come over. It'll be good to be together, and besides, Titan thinks Stormy is hilarious."

Stormy was Bo's adopted Calico cat, and she lived up to her name. She'd wreaked havoc in my house the few times I'd cat-sat her, but I couldn't refuse, because she and Coal were fast friends. Although my 166-pound Dane had initially been scared to death of the feline fluffball, they'd worked out some kind of unspoken agreement where she was in charge, and his duty was to bring her toys and other offerings of gratitude. To my horror, once he had grabbed a dead bird from the garden, hid it in his mouth, then brought it inside and deposited it next to her cat tower. She had rewarded him with several nose bats and a brief side cuddle.

"Stormy's been in rare form lately, prowling around like a panther in front of the windows. She needs some fresh entertainment," Bo said. "I'll see you around six, then."

He headed back to work, and I walked over to join Titan, who was now standing next to the brick divider wall and watching the shelter dogs.

"Did you find one you want?" I gave him a friendly nudge.

"I wish I could." His tone was gloomy. "If only my condo allowed dogs."

I looked up at his face and realized his pensive mood had nothing to do with the rules at his condo. He was still trying to work through what had become of Darby.

"Maybe we could take Coal for a walk," I suggested. "It would clear our heads a little, and he'd love it."

He gave me an appreciative look and took my hand in his. "There's nothing I'd like better."

4

As I'd predicted, Coal was eager to get on the leash the moment I mentioned the word "walk." He even went so far as to do a half-jump in front of me—he knew better than to jump up fully, because one time he'd knocked me over that way, and he still felt deep remorse for it.

He strode in front of us as we walked down the sidewalk, sniffing at the air. But I wasn't buying his confident leadership vibe—I knew he was just as easily spooked as a horse. He'd once jerked the leash from my hands and run off a short distance, only because a dry leaf had landed on his head.

Titan mused, "There's another option to consider. Darby could've been pushed. Maybe someone took the opportunity of the blackout and shoved her over."

"You mean Florence or Olivia?"

"I don't know who else it could've been."

I thought of quiet Gabe in the gift shop. "What was the cashier doing when the lights were out?"

"He told the deputies that he was behind the counter the entire time, but there weren't any customers in the shop to verify it."

"Did he know how many people were touring the cave when it happened?"

Titan shook his head. "The kid wasn't too great at the job. Although he was supposed to keep a head count of visitors touring the caverns, he admitted he'd gotten distracted when Darby and her friends came in, so he couldn't definitively say if the man who had entered the cave before our groups had exited yet."

"Could he describe the man?"

"He said he was in his forties or fifties, with graying hair. Could really be anyone. The man paid for his tour in cash." Titan shrugged.

"Well, that's not helpful—just like his story that the cavern lights went out and he didn't even realize it. I find that a little hard to believe." I pulled Coal's leash up short as a jogger passed us. He obediently sat still, tail wagging, until I gave him the go-ahead to walk again. I'd learned that Great Danes intimidated most people, no matter how well-trained they were.

We'd reached the curve in the sidewalk that led to the next street over. Titan gave me a questioning look, and I nodded. We needed more time to talk, and the sunshine and fresh air felt great.

Following up on Gabe's dubious claim he didn't know the lights went out, Titan said, "I know the cashier's story sounds suspicious, but the police verified that the gift shop power is on a different circuit from the caverns' power. The kid would've been completely unaware of what was going on in the caves."

"I suppose you're right—it was quite a hike just to get underground." I sighed. "But I find it really hard to believe that either Florence or Olivia was ready to kill Darby at the drop of the hat."

"I do, too." He stopped in front of an abandoned house, a thoughtful look crossing his handsome features. Coal took a seat on the sidewalk, politely looking up at Titan as if waiting for him to finish speaking. "There's something that's been bothering me about the stepmother, Nina," he said. "It felt like she was giving some kind of performance when the deputy explained what had happened to Darby. It didn't seem like real grief, but I can't put my finger on why."

"I think we know real grief when we see it," I observed. "I'll ask Milo for the scoop on that situation. The wicked stepmother scenario isn't limited to fairy tales, you know."

"That's what I wondered—if there was some kind of bad blood there."

We stared at the empty house in front of us. It would've been beautiful in its day, with its wraparound porch and unusual round windows tucked into the roof. But the windows were now broken and boarded up, and the porch roof was sagging.

Titan must've been thinking along the same lines. "What a waste," he said. "I know it takes a fortune to restore an old place like that. Wish I had the funds to do it."

Tired of sitting, Coal slowly stood and wagged his tail. He shot me a hopeful look, so I smiled and said, "We're going, boy."

Without further ado, he trotted off, so we had to scurry to keep up with him. As we walked by a parked green car with its windows cracked, a large black dog with a bright blue collar jumped up in the front seat, barking at us in a frenzy. Coal angled his head toward it, but didn't bark back. In this situation, I think he realized he had the upper hand.

As we were nearing my place, we ran into my neighbor Vera walking her Labradoodle, Waffles. Her short gray hair caught the rays of sunlight.

She gave us a hearty greeting. I knew she was especially fond of Titan, since she mentioned him nearly every time we talked. I was convinced she had a little cougar crush on him, although I knew she had started seeing a man her age named Randall Mathena.

Waffles was a story in and of herself. The curly-haired golden dog had been in numerous homes, only to be returned to the shelter time and time again for her crazy antics. But Vera had taken one look at her in the cafe and fallen for the fractious canine. We'd all held our breath to see if Waffles could learn to behave for the older woman, and, lo and behold, she had.

Waffles and Coal were always skittish when they got together, since their favorite pastime was barking at each other from their respective fenced yards. But today, Waffles was determined to be the better dog. She sat down and politely raised a paw, as if she were trying to shake hands with Coal.

In response, Coal scooted behind me and stood there, giving the smaller dog a look of abject terror.

Waffles repeated her hand-shaking gesture, again and again. Vera smiled. "She really wants to be friends, but Coal's having none of it, is he?"

I was glad Vera was so in tune with her doggie. Despite our pets' territorial differences, it brought so much joy to my heart to see Waffles settled into such a loving home. In fact, I was convinced that Vera needed Waffles as much as Waffles needed her. Vera had two grown children, but they lived far away and rarely came in to visit. I tried to look in on her frequently, which wasn't hard, because we always had informative conversations. Vera had been friends with my great-aunt Athaleen years ago, and she knew things about her I never would have guessed.

"We're looking forward to seeing you on Thanksgiving," I said.

She nodded. Her large brown eyes—reminiscent of my favorite dog's eyes in my teen years—always seemed so sympathetic. "I'll be bringing my famous deviled eggs and my homemade stuffing." She shot a proud look at Titan.

He gave her a respectful grin. "I can't wait. I'm hoping to make some bread—my grandma's recipe."

Vera gave a nod of approval, then turned her attention to me. As if sensing our conversation might run long, Coal finally stretched out behind my feet.

"Say, I wanted to ask you again about our book club," she began.

I knew what was coming next. I'd finagled my way out of Vera's book club for months now, but I was smart enough to know she wasn't going to let this drop. She wanted me to come and give a little presentation on the cafe—free publicity, she'd said, for her older generation of friends. She would serve our house blend coffee, and I could even sell some bags afterward, if I wanted.

It really was a win-win, but I always felt like an idiot in group settings like that. I'd visited a book club once, long ago, and it had seemed like all my hot takes on the book we discussed were way off-base. I was much more comfortable sitting in the Barks section of the cafe, surrounded by dogs, where I was in my element.

"Uh..." I glanced at Titan. I didn't want him to think I was some kind of cold-hearted neighbor, did I? "What book are you reading this month?" I stalled.

"Oh, we've already met this month. This would be our Christmas meeting, which would be an even better chance to sell coffee or any other cafe tchotchkes you might have. And we're discussing *Vanity Fair* by Thackeray. It's a whopper, but so far, it's been a fairly fast read for me."

"I enjoyed that one," Titan offered. "That one movie adaptation was also pretty accurate."

Vera's smile couldn't get any wider as she patted Titan on the arm. "A modern man who reads. Delightful."

Leaving off her friendly overtures with Coal, Waffles seemed to decide that if her owner liked Titan, she should get to know him, too. She sashayed over and began sniffing at his jeans.

Vera's voice suddenly turned commanding. "No. Sit down right now, Waffles."

So many of us, in both the cafe and the shelter, had tried using a similar tone at various times to get Waffles to obey. It had always been a hopeless endeavor, leaving us wondering if the doodle was really that ignorant or if she was some kind of anti-human rebel.

But when Vera spoke, the curly dog listened. Waffles actually took a polite seat in front of Titan and raised a paw.

Titan ruffled the hair behind her ears. Coal gave a sorrowful groan behind me, unhappy his special friend had deigned to acknowledge the dog next door.

"She's become a changed dog with you," I said.

Vera gave a quick nod, but she hadn't forgotten her original mission. "So, what do you think?" she pressed. "Could you join us for book club? You could bring some of your younger friends, too. We could use some fresh blood."

Darting a final glance at my boyfriend, I knew I'd be disappointed with myself if I didn't accept. It would get Vera off my case about it, so I might as well make the best of it.

"Sure. I'll get some cute Christmas baskets together to sell, too. Charity could bake some cookies, and Bristol could fancy up the baskets. She's great at artsy things like that."

Vera took my hands in hers. "Oh, that would be lovely! I can't wait for you to meet my friends." She stopped short. "Well, all but one of them."

Obviously, there was some kind of backstory going on here. "Who do you mean?"

She heaved a heavy sigh. "Matilda Crump, that's who. She moved to town last year and immediately jumped into every civic organization she could. She fancies herself an aficionado on all things British, since her dead husband's mother hailed from Hampshire, England, and Matilda visited there once." She shook her head. "Yes—*once*. Anyway, she's rather exasperating, but I can't exactly kick her out of the club. A reader is a reader."

I chuckled to myself at Vera's succinct rundown on Matilda. I'd have to keep my eyes open for this thorn in Vera's side when I came to the club.

Titan's phone buzzed, and he glanced at it. "I guess I'd better say goodbye for now. Nice to see you, Vera." Glancing at me, he said, "If you don't mind, I'll head over and take this call on your porch."

"Sure. I'll be over soon."

As Titan strode off, Coal's longing eyes followed him. He didn't want to miss a minute with Titan, his friend who —like him—was rather gigantic for his "breed."

"I should get back, too." I gave Vera a hug. "I'll read up on *Vanity Fair*, so I'll be prepared for all your tough questions."

She laughed. "Oh, hon, trust me. I'm lucky if I even get anyone to participate in the discussions—besides Matilda, who is always quite vocal. Just having your fresh face in my sitting room will be an encouragement. I'll see you on Thursday."

Vera led Waffles toward their fenced yard, and I told Coal it was time to go. As he walked toward my gate, he kept glancing back, as if he suspected Waffles might attempt a sneak attack on him. I had to laugh as I pictured Waffles whipping out her ninja moves and leaping onto Coal's back.

Titan was slipping his phone into his jeans pocket when I climbed the steps to my back porch. "That was the sheriff. He said they've been using the rescue dogs to search the creek, but they've had no success." He paused. "He also mentioned that word has gotten around that Darby's step-mother is already asking about the will. She's specifically wondering who will get the family home—which the sheriff tells me is gigantic."

"That goes beyond cheeky." I was feeling a wee bit British myself.

"It does. Suffice it to say, she's put herself on the police radar."

"I'll text Milo now to see what he knows about Nina. If anyone has the inside scoop on the sordid side of the upper crust, it'll be him."

5

We headed over a little early to eat at Bo's, since —as usual—he was running ahead of schedule. He'd prepared a mouthwatering meal of lemon chicken, parmesan risotto, and spinach salad. Since Summer and Titan basically felt like family, our conversation was enlightening and occasionally gut-bustingly hilarious.

Summer served mini lemon cream pies in tiny Mason jars for a light dessert. Although she said the scrumptious pies were easy to put together, I doubted I'd be able to produce a similar result if I attempted to make them.

As Summer and I washed up the dessert jars in Bo's spacious sink, she informed me that Sadie, the winsome little brindled dog that I'd met earlier in the cafe, had been adopted. "She was truly one of the smartest dogs we've ever had at the shelter." Summer displaced bubbles with her cleaning brush as she shoved it into a jar. "I kid you not, she had the sassiest look on her face when I brought her back to the shelter after her visit to the cafe. It was like she'd seen the other side, and she wasn't about to go back into a kennel. But then her new owner showed up to adopt her, and she was all high fives and doggie kisses with her."

"I'm so thrilled we've had another successful placement through Barks & Beans." I glanced at Bo and Titan, who were sitting on the couch, their heads tipped toward each other as they murmured in low voices.

"They're probably talking about that poor girl who fell in the cavern," Summer observed. "You were there, Macy. What do you think happened?"

Coal, who had been an absolute angel since we got here, came over and situated himself in an out-of-the-way corner of the kitchen. I figured Stormy, who was perched on her cat tower like the queen of Lewisburg, had worn him out. They'd been nosing and batting around a ball while we ate.

"I'm not sure," I admitted. "I can't say I have any kind of gut feeling about it, just that Darby was completely foolish to go past the railing to get a selfie."

Summer's tan nose wrinkled. "What a sad reason to throw your life away." I could hear a bit of disdain in her tone, and I recalled that she had grown up Mennonite, so her dislike for social media made sense. Although we had talked a little about her upbringing, she'd never been very forthcoming about the restrictions she'd been under as a child. What I did know was that, at some point, she'd turned her back on her upbringing, so she hadn't seen her four brothers or her parents in years.

My phone rang, so I quickly dried my hands and looked at the screen. It was Milo. After gesturing to Summer that I needed to talk, I picked up and walked down the short hallway into Bo's sunroom, which was filled with plants and wicker furniture like the rest of his beach-feel bungalow.

"Hi, Macy—uh—Miss Hatfield."

Chuckling at Milo's difficulty in calling me the more respectful name we'd asked all our employees to use, I settled into a chair. "Hey there. Did you get my text about Nina?"

"I did. I asked my friend Briggs about it, since he's been close to Darby and her family his whole life. It turns out that Darby's father Victor left her the bulk of his fortune, as well as their large house, when he died. He also left a small yearly sum to his second wife, Nina. Rumor has it that he suspected Nina was having an affair with someone, but he wasn't able to prove it. Most people figure her lover was Lamont Styles, because she married him only six months after Victor's death." He took a breath. "And here's where it gets weird. According to Briggs, Darby has been allowing Nina and Lamont to live in the house. Briggs keeps encouraging Darby to kick them out since they don't even pay her rent, but every time she tries, Nina guilt-trips her into letting them stay just a little longer."

I was surprised to hear Darby could be so gullible. She'd come off as rude and snobby in the cafe, then again in the gift shop—until I'd explained I was a co-owner of the cafe. "That's odd that she would let them stay, don't you think?"

"It's certainly unlike her," Milo agreed. "She's not what you'd call a philanthropist. I asked Briggs about it, and his hypothesis is that Nina must be holding something over Darby's head. He can't imagine what, though."

"Maybe he's not as close with Darby as he'd like to think," I said. "Does she usually confide in him?"

"That's the thing—she does, so he can't understand why she always keeps this part of her life quiet. Every time he goes over to visit, she practically tiptoes around her own house to stay out of her stepmom's way."

"That makes no sense," I said. "Darby holds all the power here."

"At least she acts like she does," he said.

Curious about Briggs' relationship with Darby, I asked, "Was Briggs the boyfriend you'd mentioned Darby recently broke up with?"

Milo laughed. "He wishes. No, he's been obsessed with Darby since first grade, but she's never been attracted to him as more than just friends."

"That's harsh." I paused. "But what do you mean about him being obsessed?"

"I know the dark way you're thinking, and you're way off-course. Briggs isn't some kind of stalker, and he wouldn't hurt a fly. In fact, I think that's why Darby didn't like him. He never could stand up to her, so she had no respect for him."

I probed a bit more. "Then who was her boyfriend? Did he have enough pluck to suit her?" Again, a British-y word had invaded my vocabulary.

"What on earth is 'pluck?'" Milo scoffed. "I assume you're talking about toughness, and sure, her ex had plenty of that. Too much, if what Briggs suspected is right."

"You mean he thought her ex hurt her?"

"Let's put it this way—both Sterling Caldwell and Darby Whitmore were accustomed to getting what they wanted, when they wanted. Put two spoiled brats like that together, and you've got a real powder keg."

Some might wrongly assume that Milo himself was a

bit of a spoiled brat, but I admired the way he'd chosen to get a job at our cafe when there was no financial motivation to do so. When we'd asked him in his interview why he wanted to work for us, he'd explained that he felt better being a contributing member of society. He didn't think that attending his parents' and friends' upscale galas and parties qualified.

Titan ducked his head under the low doorframe—something he was constantly doing, given his height. He smiled and mouthed a goodbye.

I held up a palm so Titan would wait. "I'll talk more at work tomorrow," I told Milo. "Thanks for your help. I need to run."

Titan and I headed back into Bo's kitchen together. Summer had already gone home, since she would be loading and driving shelter dogs to the cafe early in the morning. Since I was the one who would be greeting her tomorrow and getting the dogs settled in the Barks section, I needed to get home, as well. But first, I caught Bo and Titan up on what Milo had shared with me.

"Our Milo's a real wealth of information," Bo said. "Good thing we have one contact among the lives of the rich and famous around here."

I shot him a look. "You could hang out with that crowd, if you wanted. You're certainly not poor, retiring early as vice president of Coffee Mass like you did. I know the position was largely a front for your DEA work, but it did pay you handsomely."

"I don't like putting on airs." The tops of Bo's cheeks tinted a little under his freckles, but his red stubble beard hid the rest of his embarrassed flush. He *really* didn't like it when I mentioned he was loaded, even around his bud

Titan, who was already well aware of that fact. How else could Bo have afforded to renovate Auntie A's house into a gorgeous cafe?

Titan cleared his throat, probably to draw attention away from Bo's discomfort. "Thanks for the info, Macy. I know you have to work tomorrow, but is it okay if I drop in for lunch with you? I'd like to help the search team until then."

I leaned into him, and he wrapped an arm around mc. "You don't have to ask me for permission to help," I said. "It's your vacation. I'm just sorry you have to spend so much of it helping the police."

"I'd feel worse if I didn't."

Bo nodded at Titan as if he understood. "I'm off tomorrow. I'll be prepping some things for Thanksgiving, but call me if you need more hands on deck, brother," he said.

It always warmed my heart when Bo called Titan "brother," or vice versa. They'd certainly grown as close as brothers when Bo had worked in the DEA, so at this point, they had an instinctual understanding of each other. Knowing that Bo unreservedly approved of Titan was reassuring to me, especially since he'd never gotten a chance to meet my ex-husband Jake before we'd rushed to the altar. I now knew for a certainty that Bo never would've approved of Jake—in fact, I still wondered what he'd do if he ever came face-to-face with my cheating ex. Jake the Snake, as I called him, hadn't been in touch with me since September, after he'd slithered into town while Bo was gone and tried to hoodwink me out of some valuable shares of stock.

I called Coal to my side, and he slowly roused from the kitchen tile. Stormy had definitely tired him out. After making a slow and deliberate loop in front of her cat tower, presumably in case she wanted to get down and give him a goodbye rub (she didn't), he came to my side and gave a happy tail wag.

I hugged Bo, then Titan led the way toward my place, which was just a couple of houses down. I'd forgotten to leave my porch light on, so he walked me up to my door. As Coal did his nightly business in the back garden, Titan said goodnight and gave me a sweet kiss. Coal loped up the steps, and I let him into the house before giving Titan a parting wave and locking the door behind us. I appreciated his gentlemanly way of waiting until I was safe inside before he left—like Coal, Titan had nothing to worry about if some miscreant was hiding in the darkness. I was fairly certain he knew hundreds of ways to kill someone, not even counting the concealed weapon he usually carried.

Before heading up to change, I rummaged through Auntie A's bookshelves. She'd collected some leather-bound classics over the years, and, sure enough, *Vanity Fair* was one of them. I toted the book upstairs, tossing it on my bed before digging pajamas out of my drawer. As I changed, Coal kneaded his pillow at the foot of my bed exactly three times before cuddling up on it. He never deviated from this standard bedtime routine, and it always left me wondering how his doggie brain was able to correctly calculate three kneads every night.

"You're a smartie, that's what," I said, giving Coal a final pat on the head. He gave a satisfied grunt of acknowledgement and closed his eyes.

I crawled into bed, quickly pulling the quilts over me. The night had turned quite cold—in fact, I would guess it was now below freezing, given the overactive gurgling noises my hot water radiators were making.

I hated to think of where Darby might be right now. If, by some miracle, she'd managed to survive her steep fall, as well as an unbridled tumble into the stream, it seemed strange that she hadn't yet made her way home or, at the very least, to the parking lot at the caverns. Could she be wandering around in the woods, wet and chilled to the bone in her satin shorts and sleeveless blouse, wondering where or even who she was? I knew amnesia was rare, but after a fall like that, anything was possible.

I cracked open the book, hoping it was relatable enough to take my mind off my worries. When I read the subtitle, *A Novel without a Hero*, I couldn't help but smile. Maybe Thackeray had a sense of humor, after all.

Three chapters whizzed by, and I found myself entranced by Rebecca Sharp's boldness, a stark contrast to her friend Amelia's timidity. But my eyelids started drooping of their own accord, so I set the book on my night table and flipped off the lamp. As I was drifting to sleep, I got a sudden image of Darby, running through the woods in an 1800s dress. She kept looking behind her, then someone whispered in my ear, "She'll get what's coming to her."

I turned to see Olivia, with her dark hair cascading around her, an evil grin plastered on her face. As I struggled to get to sleep afterward, I couldn't shake the lingering conviction that Darby's fall was no accident.

6

Tuesday morning seemed to come too soon, so it took some serious effort to drag myself out of my warm bed. When I walked onto the porch to let Coal out, tiny snowflakes drifted onto my face and coat. I threw a glance at the street next to my house and was happy to see it hadn't gotten slushy yet. If the roads stayed clear, business in the cafe wouldn't be affected.

Once I'd opened the cafe, I puttered around, tidying up the Barks section as Kylie came in to open the Beans section. We exchanged desultory greetings, but it was obvious we both needed a couple more cups of coffee to start functioning at full capacity.

On the other hand, Summer was bright as a sunflower when she showed up, leading the shelter dogs in. She wore a multi-patterned grass green skirt and an orange sweater that really shouldn't match, but looked tropical and eclectic. Her long, caramel-colored hair was swept up into a loose bun, and her fringed earrings swept her shoulders.

Kylie, whose own dark bob was fluffed up on one side

like she'd slept on it wrong, gave Summer a dark look. "Why do you have to look so amazing this early in the morning?" she asked. "It makes the rest of us look bad."

Summer laughed. "I'm only a morning person when I get plenty of sleep, like I did last night. Then I feel like I can tackle the world. And you never look bad, Kylie. Just...slightly intimidating."

Kylie grinned. "I'll take that as the compliment I know you intended." Our heavily tattooed barista could come off as rather fierce, given her combat boots and blunt demeanor, but she was also a sweetie at heart. She had basically been a mother to her teen sister for many years, and she still worked to provide for her as much as for herself.

"You still dating Joel?" Summer asked.

Kylie blushed. Joel was a Ren Faire friend of hers who'd turned boyfriend not too long ago. He was adorably nerdy, and adorably besotted with Kylie.

"Yes. He's coming in for Thanksgiving—we're going to do a meal at my parents'. I'm not sure how that will go, but I figured he might as well know where I come from."

Where Kylie came from was a pair of alcoholic parents who now swore they were recovered. For Kylie and her sister's sakes, I hoped that was true.

Summer walked the dogs over, giving them a moment to sniff me before she unclipped their leashes. It was something I'd requested she do each time she brought new dogs in. They needed to get a feel for me and to sense that I was in charge of this space. While they sniffed, I didn't pet them or meet their eyes, I simply talked with Summer. Once they were off-leash, if they were interested in me, they'd make their way over, and *then* I would give them the attention they were looking for. It was a technique I'd learned years ago, when dealing with fractious neighbor dogs.

"These two are a bit frisky," she explained as the small dog raced toward the toy bin. "They're pretty young. The tiny one—we call him Oscar—is full-grown, but he still chews everything like a puppy. Just a heads-up for anyone interested in adopting."

"Gotcha. And what's the name of the other one?"

"We're calling her Jenga. She's sweet, but watch her, since she does need more potty breaks than most. The vet said she must have a small bladder, so I'm thinking she might make a better outdoor dog."

"That would work well with her thick coat," I observed. "I'll walk her frequently. Thanks, Summer."

She leaned closer, her brown eyes filled with concern. "Any word on Darby today? It was so cold last night."

I shook my head. "I haven't heard anything from Titan yet, but I'm not sure how early he was heading out to search."

"Keep me posted," she said. "I'm going to see if Kylie can fix me a house blend before I get back to work. Have a great day, Macy."

"You, too, my friend."

As she walked off, I looked out the large window. The heavy, steely gray cloud on the horizon warned that the weather would only get worse. Snowfall had already picked up, and the roads were getting covered. I hoped the snowplow trucks could keep up with it.

It was, in fact, the worst possible time for Darby to go missing, and I prayed she would show up today.

AROUND NOON, I was surprised to see a familiar curly red head coming in the cafe door. I headed over to greet Florence, giving her a warm hug.

"I'm so glad you came!" I walked her to the counter and asked Kylie to give her a caramel latte, on the house.

As Florence tugged off her knit cap, I took a better look at her. She had dark circles under her eyes, and her cheeks were pale and drawn. "Thanks for the coffee," she murmured. "I just needed to get out of the house, so I thought I'd drop in."

"Are you hungry? I'll cover your meal, too," I offered.

She shook her head. "I haven't been able to eat. We'd planned to go out to eat after the caverns...I just can't stomach anything."

"At least take something with you." I asked Kylie to bag up one of Charity's prosciutto croissant sandwiches that had been selling like hotcakes.

"I'd be happy to." Kylie's tone was gentle. She probably realized I'd taken the distraught Florence under my wing. "I'll put it in the fridge, so be sure to pick it up before you leave."

As if in a daze, Florence took her latte, which Kylie had adorned with a foam-art swan, and trailed me over to the Barks section. The sight of the dogs did seem to perk her up a little, and she sat down to sip her coffee.

I took a seat nearby. "My friend Titan is out searching for her. He said they have lots of community volunteers today, and the fire department is handing out hot chocolate to keep everyone warm."

"How kind," she said.

Oscar came over and rolled around near Florence's boots. She petted behind his ears for a brief moment, then he jumped back up to retrieve a ball. I was struggling with what to say next, knowing the topic of Darby was an emotional minefield for Florence.

Remembering my weird dream or vision or whatever it was, I asked, "Have you heard from Olivia?"

Florence gave an almost imperceptible frown. "No, but she's not likely to call me. She's very busy in her business."

I got the feeling that although Olivia was Darby's friend, she wasn't really Florence's. Maybe there was some kind of jealousy dynamic going on there.

"So, I guess those two got along fine?" I ventured.

She hesitated. "Most of the time. Not so much lately."

I didn't want to be that nosy person who kept asking questions, but if there was some kind of animosity between Darby and Olivia, the police needed to be aware of it—especially since Olivia was in the caves the day Darby fell. "Did you know why they were having issues?" I asked, trying to sound offhand.

Florence stared out the window at the snow, which was now pouring down. "I guess it was because Olivia was getting kind of close with Darby's ex-boyfriend, Sterling."

"You mean she stole him from Darby?"

"Oh, no, nothing like that." She took a sip of coffee. "That wasn't what upset Darby."

I really didn't want to keep pushing, but it seemed important to know what had driven a wedge between Olivia and Darby. "Then why was she upset?"

Florence set her coffee cup down and her eyes met mine. Their unusual light brown shade seemed rare for a redhead. "I can't really say."

I couldn't tell if that meant she simply didn't *want* to say, or she didn't know in the first place.

Jenga was sniffing out the side door, so I stood. "I'd better take this one for a walk. Thanks for chatting. I hope you enjoy the rest of your coffee, and don't forget to pick up your sandwich on the way out. You won't regret it."

"Thank you," she said. "I'm sure I'll come back here soon. This latte is amazing."

After clipping the leash on Jenga, I put on my coat and gloves and headed into our fenced side yard. The wind was swirling, so I had to pull my faux fur-trimmed hood up. Jenga hadn't taken three steps before she started using the bathroom, so it was a good thing I'd gotten her out when I did. We'd had accidents in the Barks section before, of course, but they were never fun to clean up.

As I rubbed my gloved hands together, I thought about Olivia's developing relationship with Sterling. Milo would likely know something about it. I decided to text him as soon as Florence left.

MILO RESPONDED to my text with a call. "It'll be easier to explain things to you on the phone, although I know you prefer text. Are you an introvert or what?"

I laughed and tossed Oscar a toy. "More of an introvert than you, I'll bet." I'd never really considered the question. While I could certainly strike up conversations on my own and I didn't shy away from human interaction, I didn't seek it out, either.

"Introverts get their energy from being alone," Milo patiently explained. "Extroverts get it from being with people."

"I don't love public speaking," I said, thinking of my looming book club engagement.

"That's actually a misconception," he said. "Some introverts excel at public speaking. The issue is more about how draining or restorative it is for you to interact with a lot of people. *Anyway*, getting down to the topic at hand—yes. Olivia is seeing Sterling. I asked Briggs, and he said that soon after Darby dumped him, Olivia pounced."

"That's caused hard feelings, I'd imagine. Florence said their friendship was a little strained."

"You've been talking with Florence?" Milo sounded shocked.

"Why—is it abnormal to talk with Florence?" I asked.

"She's just kind of a loner, even though she always runs with Darby's pack. She doesn't really talk with anyone but Darby. I think she feels uncomfortable in our circles."

"You mean wealthy people make her uneasy? I can't imagine."

"I know sarcasm when I hear it," Milo says. "I just mean she doesn't come from money. Her dad left when she was young, and her mom moved away when Florence went to college."

"That's sad. Darby is all she has left, I guess."

"And Darby's a sad excuse for a friend, if you ask me...although Briggs would tell you all about how thoughtful and witty she is. I think she's a total narcissist and uses people to get what she wants."

"Still...it would be sad if she'd died in that fall."

"Of course. By the way, they're planning a prayer vigil for her tomorrow night at the Methodist church—if they don't find her first. Briggs and I are planning to go. Do you want to join us?"

It would give me a chance to support Florence, who would doubtless be alone, and to observe Darby's friends and family more closely. "Sure."

After hanging up with Milo, I absently petted Jenga's head. Florence was basically an outcast in the social strata her best friend lived in. I wondered if any men in those circles would even consider dating her, given her less-than-affluent family status. I determined I'd look out for her during this ordeal, since no one else would.

TITAN SHOWED up at the cafe around three for a late lunch. Leaf bits were strewn in his curls, and his coat and jeans were streaked with dried mud.

I headed into the cafe to greet him. Kylie shot me a pitying look as if to say, "Your poor man has been through the wringer."

I carefully gave him a side-hug while he waited for his food. "What'd you get?" I asked, curious to see which of Charity's sandwiches he chose.

"Two of the French onion sliders," he said. "They sounded amazing—and warm. I'm used to being outside in the weather, but when I get wet and *then* cold, it seems to bite into my bones."

"Go sit by the fire. I'll pick up your food."

Bo had installed a gas fireplace next to the white brick wall, and it brought an extra touch of coziness to the cafe. Titan was only too happy to follow my instructions. He sat close to the flames and stripped off his coat. As Kylie set his coffee and sandwiches on the counter, I caught her checking out the way his wide shoulders filled out his navy

Henley shirt. She met my eyes and winked. Like most women, she couldn't help but appreciate his build, but I knew she wasn't interested in him in the slightest. Sometimes I still wanted to pinch myself that a man of Titan's caliber would be interested in me, but he was also one of the humblest men on earth and completely unaware of his powers of attraction. Plus, he truly seemed to love me for *me*—the person I was as a child, a teen, and an adult—the essence of me, really—and it was truly marvelous.

I set his food down. "I'll check on the dogs and then be right back," I said, hoping to give him some space to decompress and eat.

A woman was sitting in the Barks section, petting Jenga. Thankfully, I'd just given Jenga a little potty break, so hopefully she would be able to enjoy her bonding session.

Oscar was tearing around in circles, as if his energy reserves hadn't gotten a bit depleted after all his playing. I couldn't handle a dog like that, but he'd be exactly what some people were looking for. I opened the gate and tossed the ball to him a few times, then I gave both him and Jenga a doggie treat. I spoke briefly with the woman, who seemed to find Jenga delightful, and I gave her a heads-up about the dog's need for frequent bathroom runs.

After cleaning my hands, I headed back to the cafe. Titan had already eaten one sandwich and was starting in on the other. He dabbed his lips with a napkin and gave me a look of sheer rapture.

"Please tell Charity she's outdone herself with these things. The beef, the rolls, the flavor...it's like a work of art."

I smiled and sat down. "I will. So, I take it there's still no news on Darby?"

His smile faded. "No, and we've had the tracking dogs

out today, as well as the state police. News crews were around, too. The dogs can't seem to pick up her scent, which would make sense if she's been in the water." He took a long sip of coffee. "Oh, and Darby's stepmother showed up today with her new husband—Lamont, I think his name is. I'm pretty sure she was putting on a show for the media. She stood near the cameras, sobbing her head off, but neither she nor her husband made any effort to actually *search* for Darby."

"Grandstanding." I cringed. "How tasteless."

"Exactly. Not the most motherly stepmother." He took a deep breath as he polished off his second sandwich. "I think I'll head back to my cabin and get a much-needed shower. You said we'd eat at your place tonight?"

I nodded. "I figured we'd keep things low-key, since you've had a long day. I'll order Chinese, and we can watch a movie or something."

"Sounds like the break I need. I'd give you a hug, but I know I'm filthy." He blew me a kiss instead, then stood. "I'll see you at six."

I wondered if Nina or Lamont would speak at the prayer vigil for Darby tomorrow night. It was really sad that Nina would feel the need to pull the media focus onto herself, even as the police were actively searching for her stepdaughter. At best, it seemed inconsiderate, and at worst, it was downright disturbing.

It would almost seem as if Nina knew that Darby wasn't coming back. And, if that were the case, she could have been involved in her fall.

7

In hopes of having another adventure that wouldn't go downhill—literally—like our cavern expedition, I headed over to Titan's cabin Wednesday morning to boat around the large pond on the property. I'd packed a picnic for us to eat afterward—either outside on the deck if it turned warm, or inside the cabin, which Titan said had a wood-burning fireplace.

The sun had streaked the sky with fiery shades of red and peach as I followed the long, winding drive to the cabin. I pulled up to the garage door, and Titan walked out to greet me. He was wearing a green and navy flannel shirt, a knit beanie hat, and hiking boots. He resembled a lumberjack, and when he opened my car door and gave me a hug, he smelled like wood smoke.

It was the most irresistible combination, and I gave him a warm hug, soaking in the solid feel and smell of him.

Then he said the magic words. "Would you like a fresh cup of coffee? I've just brewed some in my French press."

I felt like I was living in a dream where all my favorite

things—the woods, an honest and loving man, and coffee —had been expertly woven together and handed to me on a platter. All that was left was a dog and some great food, and I'd brought some of Charity's sandwiches in Auntie A's well-used picnic basket.

"I'd love a cup. Thank you."

He took the picnic basket and carried it into the kitchen, where he set it on the counter. "Do I need to put anything in the fridge before we go out on the pond?"

"Only the sandwiches."

As he busied himself with the sandwiches and coffee, he said, "I didn't realize that my FBI friend Julius would be getting here around noon. He's leaving earlier than I thought. Hopefully it won't interrupt our picnic."

"We can eat a little early. I mean, shoot, you know me—I could eat anytime." I wandered around the quaint cabin, touching the spines of the thrillers lining the bookshelves. "Have you read any of these?" I asked, suddenly curious as to what kinds of reads Titan preferred.

"I have. I don't read fast, though. I have the kind of dyslexia that makes the letters look like they're jumping around on the page."

"Oh, I'm sorry—I hadn't even realized you had dyslexia."

He shrugged, adding cream to my coffee without asking, which I found adorable. He already knew what I liked. "I've gotten better at reading over the years. In school, my teachers thought I was dumb."

The idea of teachers making my brilliant man feel incompetent made my blood boil. "That's so wrong!"

He glanced up, realizing I was upset. "Oh, it worked out for the best. In the third grade, Mom pulled me out of school and started homeschooling me. She made sure I always had the most interesting books around to read—science, history, classics—so my reading rapidly improved. I still take longer than others, but I pace myself better, so I can process most of the words."

He brought my coffee over, and I sat down on the leather couch to enjoy it. He settled next to me with his own mug, his long legs extended so his ankles crossed under the coffee table.

"Your mom sounds so smart," I said. "I've wanted to meet her for awhile, so I'm glad she'll be visiting us at Christmas." I tucked my legs under me on the couch. "But tell me more about your friend Julius. You said he's an agent, looking into a connection between some stolen artwork and Anne Louise?"

"Exactly. Julius has been keeping an eye on some shady dealings of late. He's got a good vantage point, living on a houseboat up in Point Pleasant. Artwork has been moving across the Ohio River near there, and the authorities inform him when they stumble onto it."

"We're talking big-ticket items?" I asked.

"High end. Black market. But Julius is plugged in." He twisted his mug in his hands, and I had to grin as I noted the "King of the Woods" logo on the side.

"He sounds very good at his job."

"Julius is one of a kind—a real art expert—and someone I really respect. You'll enjoy meeting him." He drained his mug and said, "You ready to get out on the pond? It's an older rowboat, but that'll make this a real adventure."

"It hasn't frozen over or anything? The past few days have been cold."

"I checked on it this morning. Only the outer edges were a little icy, and they were already melting. It's a fairly deep pond. Just be sure you dress really warmly."

"Definitely." My mind once again flew to poor Darby and her shorts and sleeveless top. "That reminds me—there's a prayer vigil for Darby tonight at the Methodist church. Do you want to come along with me?"

"I would, but Julius was planning on staying for dinner tonight. He's bringing some grass-fed beef with him, and he says he'll grill up the best burgers I've ever had." He chuckled.

"Men and their grills," I said. "No problem. I'll let you know how the vigil goes, and you keep me posted on how the police search goes."

"They're dragging parts of the river today." His voice was quiet as he slipped an arm into his coat. "Although the community has stepped up to search along the creek and river, I have this feeling she's not there. I still can't understand how the dogs wouldn't have picked up on anything."

Neither did I. And with every day that passed, the slim hope that Darby might have survived her fall dwindled.

AFTER HAVING a relaxing but slightly damp time in the leaky rowboat, we headed inside to warm up with our indoor picnic. Julius Vos arrived just as we were finishing up our food. He turned out to be a handsome, white-haired man with some of the sharpest eyes I'd ever looked into. If "eyes are the windows to the soul," I felt fairly certain Julius could see right into mine. It made me glad we were on the same team in regard to the whole Anne Louise situation. If we could tear down the entire Moreau crime empire and send Anne Louise to join her husband behind bars, so much the better for West Virginia, in my opinion.

I headed home around one, and, after running to the grocery store and taking care of a few errands, it was time to shower and get ready for the vigil. As was his habit, Coal stretched out along the outside of the bathroom door once I'd closed it behind me. I figured something deep inside told him I was in a vulnerable position in that room, and he wanted to make sure no one snuck up on me.

I figured black was not the cheeriest color to wear to a vigil for a missing person, so I chose my favorite Persian blue blouse and paired it with navy pants. I wasn't sure the shades matched, but I didn't have time to second-guess myself, since Milo was coming to pick me up. He'd insisted on driving, and had promised to introduce me to anyone I had questions about.

In a flurry, I added a pair of dangly earrings Summer had given me, then pulled on my brown heeled boots. I raced downstairs, first checking on Coal's water dish, then locking up before going outside.

Milo's silver Porsche Turbo sedan was parked along my sidewalk. Its engine was running, but I couldn't even hear it until I got right next to the car. Milo had jumped out, and he opened the passenger door for me.

"Well, aren't you gallant today?" I asked, settling into the white leather seat.

"I try." He closed my door before heading around the front. After sliding into his seat, he put the car in gear and made an impossibly tight U-turn on our small street. He shot me a devilish grin.

My eyes played over his choice of clothing this evening.

As usual, he was the picture of sophistication. He wore chinos, a light blue shirt, a green striped tie, and an unbuttoned navy blazer. There were no logos in sight, but the tailored look of his outfit told people he not only fit in with local society—he ruled it. Not to mention his tortoiseshell Ray-Bans, which reminded me of the East Egg lot in *The Great Gatsby*.

As he whirred down the streets like a bullet out of a gun, he said, "You look fine, in case you're wondering. I know you tend to get awkward at these kinds of events."

"Excuse me? Just because I've occasionally asked you what to wear doesn't mean I'm *completely* inept," I protested.

"Mm-hm." His tone was laced with disbelief.

He was a sassy little so-and-so, as Auntie A would've called him, but I knew he had a heart of gold. Plus, he liked Bristol, which showed that no matter how important his parents were (what *did* they do, exactly?), he had his head screwed on straight. Bristol was just as gorgeous, real, and selfless as they came.

Milo had to maneuver his car into a tiny spot on the edge of the block, since the church lot was filled. "A lot of people here tonight," I observed.

Milo's lips twisted. "That's because anyone who's anyone knows they have to show up. They have to be *seen*." He turned to me with an unexpected look of sadness. "I could count on one hand the number of people I know who are real. And Macy—I mean, Miss Hatfield—you'd better believe you're one of them."

I felt a stab of pain for my forlorn barista. Hopefully, Milo's parents made it into his "real" category...but something told me they didn't.

"Thank you, Milo."

He came around to open my door, and as I got out, a tall blond man was striding up the sidewalk, directly toward us. He gave me a nod, and I gave him a hesitant smile. Did I know him?

Walking straight over to Milo, he greeted him with, "My brother!"

Milo had a brother? How did I not know this?

The blond, who was taller, blonder, and preppier than Milo, grinned at me. "And you must be Macy Hatfield. Milo said he was bringing you tonight. It's wonderful to finally meet you—I've been planning to visit the cafe, but I just haven't gotten around to it." His smug smile seemed to say otherwise, as if cafes were beneath him. "I'm Hudson Donovan, Milo's older and infinitely wiser brother."

"Nice to meet you," I said.

Milo seemed eager to get out of this interaction. "We'd better head inside," he said.

Hudson pulled a dramatic frown. "Isn't it awful? No one can believe that Darby might be gone from us forever." His smug look, which was probably a permanent fixture, returned. "Then again, I guess Sterling might have to pay the piper now."

An attractive young woman called to Hudson from the church door, so he abruptly strode off, giving us a backhanded wave.

Milo sighed. "Sorry about that. My brother is in a league of his own." He led the way toward the church. Inside the spacious auditorium, people were standing in clusters, talking in hushed tones.

A sturdy-built guy with dark hair hurried over to Milo. "Dude, I'm so glad you're here. If Nina busts into tears one more time, I'm going to lose it." He threw a glance at me, as if realizing for the first time I was here with Milo.

Milo introduced us. "This is my friend Briggs Feinberg. Briggs, this is my boss, Macy Hatfield." He leaned in toward me and whispered, "He's one of the real ones."

Briggs gave me a genuine smile. "Miss Hatfield—Milo's told me so much about Barks & Beans. It was a genius idea. I'm in awe."

I couldn't resist his enthusiastic candor. "Thank you—it was actually my brother Bo's brainchild."

Briggs nodded and started talking to Milo in a hushed tone. "Sterling had a lot of nerve to show up," he said. "And Olivia's hanging all over him. It's disgusting."

I glanced around, wondering which one Sterling was, but it didn't take long to pick him out of the crowd. All I had to do was locate Olivia, and she was easy to spot. Not only was she taller than most of the women in her group, but she was wearing a bright pink dress that was practically the same shade of fuchsia as Darby's jacket on the day she fell. Maybe she was making some kind of warped homage to her friend, but it looked more like a stick-it-to-you move, given the fact that she'd linked arms with the tall, brown-haired man beside her. He had to be Darby's ex, Sterling.

Milo followed my gaze. As if reading my mind, he nodded. "That's Sterling Caldwell," he confirmed.

Sterling looked like Remington Steele, complete with the blazer. Quite a few of Darby's friends were gathered around him and Olivia, all chattering together like they were just waiting for a movie to begin.

Clearly, Olivia was the one who had captured Sterling's attention. He glanced over at her periodically and smiled.

"It's sickening," Briggs muttered. "I know Darby dumped him, but seriously. They act like this whole thing is a joke."

Like some kind of flaming redheaded beacon, Florence entered the church and made her way toward her group of friends. She stood awkwardly outside the circle, but after a couple of minutes, Olivia seemed to take notice of her. The brunette extended her arms in a dramatic gesture and pulled Florence closer.

But when Sterling placed a hand on Florence's shoulder, she shrank back, as if expecting him to hit her. Milo and Briggs were talking, so they probably hadn't noticed it. Was I seeing things?

8

I didn't have time to ponder Florence's unmistakable flinch, because a woman in black strode to the pulpit and grabbed the microphone. It gave a loud squeal of protest, and she tapped at it several times, which didn't help. We hurried to take our seats on a nearby pew.

"Can you hear me?" she asked.

Someone in the middle said, "Yes," so the woman continued. "I'm Nina Styles, Darby's stepmother. Thank you for gathering here tonight to pray for our precious daughter."

Briggs cleared his throat in a less-than-polite way.

"The police are still searching for Darby, and we're trying to stay hopeful that they'll find her soon," she continued. "Lamont and I wanted to say a huge thank you to everyone in town who has helped with the search." She gestured to a bulky, middle-aged man sitting on the front row who must be Lamont.

Tears began to trickle down her face. "As you know, tomorrow is Thanksgiving, and all we want is for our family to be together. If you have any information, please get it to the police. And let's keep our prayers up!" After replacing the mic in its stand, she teetered down the steps in her heels and took a seat next to Lamont.

Olivia stood up next and glided toward the pulpit, lithe as a cheetah. Her voice wavered as she said, "I was there with Darby in the caverns. She wanted to support local businesses, so we were visiting different ones. That's the kind of person she was." She made a hand gesture, and music began to play on the speaker system. Then she began to sing.

Surprisingly, she had chosen the country song "Not Forgotten," one of the best-loved hits from my friend Carolina and her band Carolina Crush. The song was wildly inappropriate for a prayer vigil, since it was a lament to a lost love, so I couldn't imagine why she'd chosen it. On top of that, Olivia didn't have the range to hit the high notes, so everyone had to suffer through the chorus in silence. A child in front of us actually flattened his hands over his ears until the music stopped.

I expected Florence to say a few words once the song concluded, but she didn't budge.

Nina stood from her seat. "That's all," she said, waving us out like we were flies.

With a furious grunt, Briggs rose from his seat and stalked up to the pulpit. He didn't even bother to grab the microphone. "I have something to say," he boomed, shooting Nina an icy look. "Darby was the best of all of us."

Milo edged from his seat and started creeping toward the stage. He must've sensed Briggs was about to go off the rails, which he promptly began to do.

Briggs stared at Olivia. "If she's dead, so help me, I'm

going to devote my life to finding out how that happened. Who cares if the caverns are a local business? If they're responsible for any injury to Darby, I'll have my dad sue the pants off them."

Milo strode toward Briggs and placed his arm around him. "He's devastated by her loss," he explained briefly. "Thank you all for coming. Have a good night." He walked his agitated friend off the stage.

The crowd began to disperse. With his face set, Milo walked Briggs straight past my pew and outside. I knew he was anxious to leave, but I wanted to check in with Florence first.

She was still seated toward the front, all alone in her little bubble. Olivia, Sterling, and the gang had already cleared out, which didn't surprise me a bit.

I sat down in the pew behind her, giving her back a comforting pat. "You doing okay?" I asked.

"I think so." She shivered, even though her well-worn blue sweater looked overly warm for the heated church building. "I just need some kind of closure, you know?"

Hudson, who'd stayed behind to talk with a friend, approached us. Florence gave him the kind of respectful nod one would give a commanding officer, which made me curious. Did she act this way toward everyone, or just Hudson?

He spoke quietly. "Florence, I'm so sorry." Turning toward me, he asked, "Did Milo already leave with Briggs? Do you need a ride home?"

"I don't really know," I said. "I guess we'd better go see what he's up to."

Nina, who had lingered behind, walked our way. Hoping to avoid meeting the rather repulsive woman, I murmured a goodbye to Florence before following Hudson outside.

Someone must've just loaded their fireplace or wood-burning stove, because wood smoke drifted our way. The air held that unmistakable tang of winter that made me want to hike in the woods, but deer hunting season was already underway.

Milo and Briggs were loitering next to Milo's Porsche. It appeared that Milo was still trying to talk Briggs down from the emotional ledge he was on.

Hudson sniffed. "That kid's always been a loose cannon, so it's no wonder he made such a dramatic speech. He's been infatuated with Darby forever, and he's not dealing with this well."

"How did you feel about Darby?" I knew Milo didn't care for her snobbish ways, but I wondered if his brother might have a different take.

Hudson stopped short, as if contemplating my question. "I can't say that I feel any particular way about her. She's younger than me, for one thing, even though she does occasionally run with my crowd."

"And what kinds of things does your 'crowd' do, exactly?"

His ice blue eyes flashed with some kind of private amusement. "You're rather a bold one, aren't you, Macy Hatfield?"

Something about the way he said my name—on my level, and not "Miss Hatfield" like his brother—didn't sit well. Of course, he wasn't my employee, so he had no reason to call me by my formal name. But it felt like he was placing himself above me, as if he had access to the upper echelons of Lewisburg and I most definitely did not.

We'd reached the Porsche, where Briggs was opening the back door.

Hudson stepped over toward his brother. "Were you taking Macy home? Did you want me to drop her off?"

Milo didn't even notice Hudson had called me by my first name—probably because he secretly thought of me as "Macy" and only used "Miss Hatfield" at my request. He shot a distracted look our way and opened the passenger door for me. "No, I'll take both of them. Thanks."

Hudson gave me a brief nod, then strode off. The moment I sat down, Briggs leaned forward. "Can you believe it? No one even prayed at the prayer vigil. Plus, Nina didn't give anyone a chance to talk, outside of herself and Olivia. Convenient, I'd say."

Milo dropped into his seat and shot Briggs a look. "I said you need to let this go. Let's talk about something else."

I knew he was embarrassed by his friend, but there must be some underlying reason for Briggs' animosity toward Olivia. Was he simply jealous that she spent more time with Darby than he did?

"I didn't really feel that song was appropriate," I ventured.

Briggs pounced. "Right? It didn't even fit the circumstances. But Olivia has always been about Olivia, first and foremost. You heard that she swiped Darby's ex-boyfriend? Some people say she was seeing him while he was *with* Darby. And now she seems to be taking over Darby's friend group, too."

Milo shot me a look that seemed to say *Don't poke the bear*.

Unfortunately, I couldn't stop myself, because I couldn't shake my instinctual distrust of Olivia. As I'd watched her working the now-leaderless clique and openly clinging to Darby's ex at the vigil, it had brought to mind Becky Sharp, that skilled manipulator of high-society friendships in *Vanity Fair*. She, too, had used people so she could climb to the top—even crushing her own friends and family along the way. Olivia seemed to have the same drive.

"How does Olivia treat Florence?" I asked.

Briggs huffed. "Even though she gave Florence a hug today, it was only a show. She never has a nice word to say to her since she comes from a different social strata."

Milo pulled up to my sidewalk and parked. He rolled his eyes, as if Briggs had completely exasperated him.

"Thanks so much for the ride, Milo. I did have a quick question for you, though," I said.

"Okay, fire away, I guess." His gaze sharpened, as if his job might hang on answering this question correctly. His eye-color was similar to my own, only a bit more on the blue side than the gray. I supposed, with my strawberry blonde hair, we might even look like siblings.

"Your brother said something about Sterling having to pay the piper now. Do you know what he meant?"

He quirked a light eyebrow. "You caught that, did you?"

Before he could elaborate, Briggs blurted, "He meant the gambling debts."

I didn't know much about gambling, but Sterling seemed awfully young to be doing it. "Is he in with some unsavory types?" I asked.

Milo surprised me with a loud laugh. "Unsavory? I guess it depends on your definition." He gave me a slanted smile. "My brother runs a little gambling club. They play for really high stakes. I guess you could say it's what the rich do when they're bored."

Briggs butted in again. "Sterling is a regular with the club, and he's always losing money. Darby told me he's dug himself into debt, and now he keeps asking her for loans—even after she broke up with him. She was really sick of it."

Now this was some *very* interesting information. I wanted to probe more, but Milo's tight-lipped look told me the topic was closed.

"Okay...well, thanks for letting me tag along tonight." I looked at Briggs. "There's still a chance they might find her. Try not to give up hope."

Briggs gave a sad shrug.

"I hope you all have a good Thanksgiving," I added, but my words seemed empty in light of the vigil we'd just attended.

"You, too," Milo said.

I closed the car door and headed through the back garden. As usual, the moment I unlocked my back porch door, Coal was on the other side, waiting to greet me with shining eyes and a thudding tail.

After giving him a thorough petting, I let him out, then went inside to scrounge up something to eat. The thought of Titan and Julius sitting around discussing criminal masterminds while eating their grilled burgers made my stomach growl. I dug up a frozen supreme pizza and turned the oven on, figuring I'd make a small salad to go along with it.

Coal bumped into the screen door, so I opened it for him. He went straight for his water bowl and started guzzling while I slid my pizza into the oven.

My text tone sounded, so I picked up my phone to see who it was.

Titan had texted, "They've interviewed a witness who

was in the parking lot that day, and she said a man came out, wearing a baseball cap and a black leather jacket. She didn't get a good look at him because he ran past her and up the driveway."

I texted back, "Where was Gabe the cashier at that time?" My phone buzzed in response, so I picked up the call.

"It'll be easier to talk this way," Titan said, picking up where our texts had left off. "Gabe said he stepped into the side room for a late lunch break, so he put the *Closed* sign up for about ten minutes to keep new customers from roaming around the shop. He was the only one there that day, since they only have two cashiers on weekends and holidays. When he returned, the lady who is our witness was knocking on the gift shop door, asking if they were open. So he can verify that she was there, but he didn't see the guy in the baseball cap."

I set my phone on the counter and put it on speaker so I could start rinsing my lettuce. "And there's no word on Darby tonight?"

"None, although the sheriff did tell me they've checked her credit cards for activity. There's been none since she fell, but she did have an airplane ticket booked to Michigan for the day after the cavern tour."

"That's interesting. I wonder who she knows up there?" As I chopped the lettuce and tomatoes, I asked, "So—how did the burgers turn out? Is Julius still there?"

"He is, so I'd better let you go. And the burgers were amazing. He used some kind of seasoning that had quite a kick to it."

"Sounds fantastic." Setting out my salad dressing, I said, "I'll see you tomorrow."

"At one, right? That'll give me plenty of time to bake my bread."

"Can't wait to taste it. Have a good night."

I prepped a big bowl of salad, planning to eat the healthier half of my supper first. When I sat down at the table, Coal sank onto his pillow to observe me from a polite distance.

I tried reading a little *Vanity Fair*, but quickly lost interest because I was still mentally rehashing the events of the vigil. From Olivia's awful solo to Nina's pretense that she loved Darby, the whole thing left a bitter taste in my mouth.

Also, the way Florence recoiled from Sterling's touch spoke louder than words. Why would she anticipate that he would hit her? Was it something from her past, or had she seen him do it before—perhaps to Darby?

9

I slept in on Thanksgiving morning, since the house was mostly decorated and all I had to do was set out Auntie A's yellow flowered china. I was only in charge of dessert, and I'd already made my pumpkin caramel trifle late last night. After painstakingly following Charity's recipe, I felt reasonably certain it had turned out okay, but just to be on the safe side, I'd also asked Charity to set aside some of her small French gingerbread cakes after work yesterday so we'd have another dessert option.

A little before one, I unlocked the door that connected my section of the house to the closed cafe. Once I'd flipped on a light, I headed for the fridge in the back room. Sure enough, Charity had left me eight cakes, which was more than enough for the five of us.

"What a sweetie," I murmured, thankful once again for our fairy godmother of baking. Each of our baristas had big hearts and were always looking out for one another.

Titan was the first to arrive, toting two loaves of fresh bread with him. "I used my Granny McCoy's recipe—hopefully you Hatfields won't take offense," he joked as he set them on the counter.

Soon after, Bo knocked on the door. He'd packed the turkey, stuffing, and mashed potatoes into a wagon and parked it at the bottom of my back steps, so Titan hurried to help him carry things in.

Summer arrived next, bringing a huge salad and green beans. Finally, Vera knocked on the door, and when I opened it, I couldn't help but grin at just how adorably fixed up she was. She wore a burgundy sweater, scarf, dress pants, and low heels. It was just the sort of outfit Auntie A would've chosen, only she'd veered more toward pastel hues.

I'd opted for comfort, wearing dark jeans and a soft blue flannel shirt, along with my yellow Harry Potter Hufflepuff socks.

Titan grinned when he caught sight of them. "You're a Hufflepuff? I guess I shouldn't be surprised. I tore through that series in high school."

"And what are you?" Bo asked.

"I'm a Slytherin," Titan said.

"A little bit dangerous," I observed. "Bo's a Gryffindor—classic hero type."

"Of course," Titan said.

I would've asked Summer what Potter house she was—and Vera, if she knew—but they were already deep in conversation in the kitchen. I quietly joined them, arranging foods on the dining table. I'd used all the leaves to extend it, but it didn't take long to pack the tabletop with food. It was a lovely problem to have. Thanksgiving was one of my favorite times of year, when we had our fill of food and good conversation.

Coal stood between Bo and Titan as they talked, his sleek head held high as if he were one of the guys. I chuckled, and Vera followed my gaze.

"Bless him," she said. "He looks like he's got something important to say. Waffles is always trying to talk to me, and I swan if some of her little barks don't sound like words."

Summer turned from the fridge, where she was grabbing the salad dressings. "You've done wonders with that dog, Vera. We were worried she'd never find a home."

"I can't explain our connection," Vera said. "But when I saw her, I knew she was what was missing in my life."

After we'd settled at the table, Bo prayed and then we began passing the dishes around. I was slathering butter on a slice of bread when Summer asked, "Is there any word on Darby?"

Vera fluttered a hand to her chest. "Oh, that poor girl."

"Nothing yet, I'm afraid," Titan said.

Bo's sky-blue gaze sharpened. "What do you think happened?"

Titan leaned back in his chair. "I honestly don't know. I've been going over the scenario in my head. We know that Darby fell from the ledge since Florence heard her body thud, and we found her cracked phone and jacket down below. But we don't know what happened afterward. My guess is that she must've bounced—or maybe she crawled or rolled in the wrong direction when she came to—and she got swept up in that swollen stream. She could have gotten wedged between the stream and the cave walls, but Search and Rescue used a thermal imaging camera soon after she fell, and there was no heat signature. She would've still been warm at that point."

"What about the guy with the baseball cap who ran out

soon after Darby fell? Do you think he could've pushed her and then booked it?" I asked.

"It certainly seems feasible." Titan ate a spoonful of mashed potatoes he'd drowned in gravy. "But who would've had a motive to do something so extreme?"

"You went to the prayer vigil, Macy," Bo said. "Did Darby have conflicts with her family or friends?"

"Plenty." I ate half a deviled egg and sighed. "Vera, these are amazing. What did you put in there?"

"My homemade carrot relish. I can a few pints every year." She folded her hands together, and I noticed she was wearing her small diamond and wedding band. She'd been widowed a few years ago, which was why she'd decided to move back to Lewisburg. But her marriage had been a happy one, unlike my great-aunt Athaleen's. Vera didn't talk about her husband Russ often, but when she did, she had nothing but good to say about him.

Summer turned her troubled eyes on Titan. "Are you thinking Darby is dead, then? What a horrible thing to happen near Thanksgiving."

"It's definitely sad timing, but I'd hesitate to guess if she's alive or dead. Sometimes these crazy situations turn out better than you'd think. We're still working to get the full picture. The sheriff is keeping me in the loop, which I appreciate."

"I'm sure he's grateful for your advice and help," I said, quietly proud of my FBI agent boyfriend.

Bo took a deep breath. "Well, I don't know about you all, but I'm ready to brew up some coffee and set out the dessert. What do you have for us, sis?"

My trifle turned out better than I'd hoped, and I wound up having two helpings. By the time everyone had finished with it, there was only a tiny portion left, which I put in a small bowl for Vera to take home.

We sat around my living room, eating dessert and sipping cappuccinos Bo whipped up for us in the cafe. Titan's long arm was draped around my back, and Coal rested next to my feet. Bo and Summer sat together in the loveseat, and Vera had chosen my low-backed chair to relax in.

I glanced around, trying to soak in one of those moments where everything was perfect in my world. I had my family and friends around me, my loyal dog nearby, a home I loved, and delicious coffee and food in hand. It was almost as if a hazy golden glow surrounded us as we enjoyed our time together.

Titan's phone rang, so he looked at the screen. When he saw who was calling, he raised an eyebrow. "It's Detective Hatcher. I'll go into the guest room to talk."

Bo heard what Titan had said, and he shot me a look. We both knew that if our friend and homicide detective Charlie Hatcher was involved, that could only mean one thing.

Darby must have been found—and she must be dead.

Titan's face was serious when he emerged from the guest room. We fell silent, waiting to hear what the detective had called about.

"This is on the complete down-low." He took a seat on the couch next to me. "It won't be publicly announced until this evening, after they've let her family know. But they've found Darby." His eyebrows drew together. "It's the strangest thing, though. Her body was discovered last night, in an abandoned house. I actually think it was the one we saw on the next street over, Macy. An older neighbor thought she heard a dog barking in there and a light was shining in an upstairs room, which didn't make sense because the house is slated to be torn down soon. So she walked up to the front porch and peered in. When she couldn't get in the front door, she went around back and found that door unlocked. I guess she then made her way upstairs, where she found Darby lying dead near a mattress. There was a half-eaten sandwich lying next to her, so they're testing it now."

"Someone poisoned her?" Bo asked.

Titan shrugged. "The detective is checking into all the possibilities. But the coroner says Darby was alive until late Tuesday night, which means she survived her fall." He stretched his legs. "Here's where it gets even weirder—there wasn't a mark on her body."

"Then how could she have fallen?" Summer asked.

Before Titan could answer, Vera gave him a thoughtful look. "Some nosy old lady living on the next street over found her, you say? Did the detective mention her name, by any chance?"

Titan pointed at her. "That's what I meant to tell you. It was that woman you'd mentioned from your book club. Mildred, was it?"

"Matilda Crump." Vera's tone was just a shade away from scornful. "She never did know when to keep to her own business. She lives on that street, and she's always imagining drug deals and mob hits are going on there."

"In this instance, I guess she was right to look into things," I pointed out.

"She could've gotten herself killed! What if it had been a drug den?" Vera made a whistling noise through her teeth. "She's tottery as everything, even with her cane. How foolish of her."

Those were some strong words, coming from Vera. Matilda certainly seemed to rub her the wrong way.

Bo seemed to be thinking aloud. "Why would Darby hole up in an abandoned house instead of returning to her own place?"

"That part's not clear," Titan said. "But someone must've brought her food and drink, since she would've been recognized if she'd picked up food in town."

"Or maybe she had a stash there...does the house belong to her?" I asked.

"Detective Hatcher checked on the deed, and he said the house belongs to the town, since it's getting torn down for a beautification project." Titan gave Coal's head a pat as he leaned against his leg.

"Someone must've brought Darby that sandwich, if they're thinking she was poisoned," Bo remarked.

"Did the police ever get Darby's phone unlocked to check her final calls?" I asked.

Titan nodded. "They did, but they found nothing out of the ordinary. Just calls to her friends and one to her stepmother. They checked her apps and photos, but found nothing disturbing, save her final selfie photo on the ledge."

Summer shook her head. "Yet another death due to popularity posting on the internet—otherwise known as taking unwise selfies." She glanced at her phone. "I'd better get on home. My parents are giving me a call today."

"I didn't realize Mennonites had phones," I said. I also didn't realize Summer even spoke with her parents. I thought they had blacklisted her when she left the community.

"They're allowed to have them, but my parents don't actually own one. They set up a time and borrow the neighbor's phone, so I'd better scoot. They only call me on holidays." She looked more defeated than I'd ever seen her, and I hated that she had such a broken relationship with her family. Bo stood to give her a kiss on the cheek, then she grabbed her bag of leftovers from the fridge and headed out.

Even though I couldn't remember much about my parents since they'd both died in a creek flood when I was two, Auntie Athaleen had stepped into the gap and adopted Bo and me. I'd never had to wonder if I was loved, because she'd given us an unshakeable sense of home and belonging. But Summer must feel her family didn't love her since she no longer shared their beliefs, and it was truly heartbreaking.

Vera stood, brushing invisible lint from her pants. "I suppose I should get home and let Waffles out," she said. She gestured toward the back door. "Summer is such a dear. What sort of parents wouldn't be proud of a girl like that? She runs that shelter singlehandedly and has a heart for saving animals. She's polite, attentive, and caring. And she has great taste in men!" She walked over and gave Bo a squeeze on his shoulder.

He grinned. "Why, thank you, Vera. And don't worry—Summer has said we're all the family she needs."

I found that pretty hard to believe, since I'd noticed she

got a little emotional talking about sibling relationships. I knew she missed her brothers.

As Vera walked my way, I stood up and pulled her into a big hug.

Her brown eyes grew teary. "Thank you again for hosting us today, Macy. It was so nice to have a reason to make my deviled eggs and cranberry sauce again. My kids haven't been home for Thanksgiving for years."

I struggled to keep my own composure. I knew Vera's daughter lived in Arizona, which would be an expensive trip, but her son lived in Georgia. He could make more of an effort to visit his mom once in awhile.

Once I'd taken Vera's leftover bag from the fridge, I located her clean dishes and tucked them into it. After letting Coal out into the back yard, I toted Vera's things down the steps for her and told her goodbye.

Bo was yawning when I came back inside. "I'm heading home for my traditional post-turkey nap. I'll come over later to divvy up our food, Macy." He gave Titan a quick hand clasp. "Thanks for coming today. Always good to see you."

As Bo left, I turned to Titan. "Was there anything you wanted to do? Or were you ready for a nap, too?"

"Actually, I was thinking a walk would be nice, since I ate way too much. You'd mentioned Sandstone Falls—would that be a good place to hike?"

Sandstone Falls was tucked between the mountains in Summers County, and there was a boardwalk trail around it. In fact, it was part of the newly-established New River Gorge National Park. I hadn't been there for some time, but I'd heard that some new restaurants had opened in the nearby town of Hinton.

"Sure. Would it be okay if we take Coal? He'd love it."

"You know I like hanging out with him."

"Excellent. And Titan—I know you weren't saying much about that sandwich lying next to Darby, but if she was actually poisoned, someone knew she was alive." Chills crawled up my arms. "Maybe even someone who showed up at the vigil last night."

10

Our hike near Sandstone Falls was quiet, since there weren't many people out. Coal tugged on his leash, sniffing at everything and acting like he was clearing the way through the jungle on our behalf.

Afterward, we headed into Hinton, which had once been a busy railroad town. Most of the shops were closed, but we found a brick-oven pizza place that was doing take-out orders, so we got a pizza to take home. I knew the warm smell of food would be tantalizing to Coal, so I gave him a couple of jerky-type treats to gnaw on as I drove.

Milo called, so I put him on speakerphone. "Did you hear the news?" he asked urgently. "They found Darby dead in an old house. They're not saying what happened, but the sheriff made a statement that they're not ruling out foul play."

So the news was out, then. "Are there any theories floating around your circles as to what happened to her?" I asked.

"Oh, yeah. Florence is convinced that Sterling crept into

that house and killed her. She told Briggs she'd seen Sterling hit Darby once, and Darby had told friends he could get violent, especially when he was drunk. In fact, Florence says that's the real reason Darby broke up with him. She was thinking about moving to Michigan to get out of his reach, actually."

This was alarming. Not only was Sterling an abusive ex-boyfriend, but, according to Briggs, he'd been harassing Darby for money to pay his gambling debts after they'd broken up. Darby was worried enough to book a flight to Michigan for the day after her cavern trip, so maybe his aggressive behavior had been escalating.

"Do *all* Darby's friends know about this?" I asked. "Otherwise, why on earth would Olivia start dating someone she knew to be physically abusive?"

"Florence said Olivia didn't believe Darby's story. She swears Sterling is a perfect angel."

Things just weren't adding up. "Does Florence have any explanation as to how Darby emerged from the caverns alive? She's the one who heard her hit the floor of the cave," I said.

Coal shifted in the back seat, staring at the phone as if he had something to add to our conversation. Titan was looking at the road, but I knew the wheels were turning lightning-fast in his mind.

Milo said, "She says she doesn't understand it. She felt sure that fall would've killed Darby. But for now, she's calling the police to tell them about Sterling's abusive behavior. She said she refuses to keep a lid on it anymore."

"She might make herself a target that way," I said. "Tell her to be careful."

"I will. Briggs is talking her through things, since they

were both so close to Darby."

I was having trouble understanding the nature of Briggs' relationship with Darby. They'd been friends for a long time, but she had no interest in him romantically. It was unclear how much time they'd actually spent together of late. Was her "friendship" simply a product of Briggs' wishful thinking?

"If you had to name one person who might be capable of killing Darby, who would you guess?" I asked Milo. Sometimes people's gut reactions weren't far from the truth —like the woman who feels an initial repulsion toward a man who turns out to be a predator. The book *The Gift of Fear* had opened my eyes to that fact.

"I'd guess Nina," he said. "I don't know who else would be next in line to inherit Darby's fortune. She had no siblings."

"Good point," I said. "Thanks for calling, Milo."

Titan and I were discussing what Milo had said when Detective Hatcher called with an update. Titan asked if it would be okay for me to listen in, since I'd helped with previous investigations in the community and I was keeping an ear to the ground in Darby's circles for any helpful information in this case. The detective agreed, saying I could fill Bo in if I wanted, but that we'd need to keep quiet about the circumstances of Darby's death until he made that public. He then went on to explain what they'd found thus far.

"Initial autopsy results are showing that Darby ingested an overdose of blood pressure medication, probably sometime Tuesday night. White powder traces of crushed antihypertensive pills were discovered between the slices of turkey on the sandwich she ate. Scene investigators lifted a beer bottle with her prints on it from the trash, which matches what the coroner found in her stomach. Apparently she drank the beer first, so it sped the blood pressure medication's effects. Her heart rate and breathing levels dropped to the point where she passed out, then died."

What a terrible way to go—all alone in some abandoned house, feeling your body slowly shutting down and knowing there was nothing you could do about it.

"She didn't have a phone on her?" I asked.

"None. Either the one we found on the floor of the cavern was her only one, or, if she had a backup, someone took it after she died."

"Obviously you haven't found anyone else's prints," Titan observed.

"Not at this point. We are going through everything in the house, but it'll take time."

"At least people can stop searching now," I said. In our small community, people didn't take a missing person report lightly. They'd keep searching far longer than advised. Thoughts of their own daughters or granddaughters would drive them to go above and beyond to find one of their own who was possibly injured or stranded out in the cold.

"It's a grim Thanksgiving for her family, I'm afraid." The detective's voice was reflective. His Thanksgiving had been interrupted, as well, but he wasn't thinking of himself.

"I'm not sure how close they really are," I commented.

"Interesting. Well, I'll be talking with them further, as well as with Darby's friends, of course." Detective Hatcher sounded discouraged. "What are you thinking, Titan? Have you seen any cases like this before? To me, it's not making sense."

Titan took a deep breath. "There *is* something that keeps coming to mind. Remember when that lady and her husband and son pretended she'd fallen over the gorge at Grandview Park over in Raleigh County? Search and Rescue, the National Guard, and everyone available searched for her for days. They rappelled down the cliffs, used thermal imaging, flew over with helicopters and drones—everything. After all that costly time and effort, police finally stumbled onto her at her home, where she was holed up in a closet with plenty of snack foods. She and her family had cooked up the story of her falling down the overlook in hopes she could avoid a prison sentence she was going to receive that month for other crimes."

"That's right, I remember that," I said. "The husband and son planted her clothing and phone at the scene, but she later admitted she'd never even been at the park that day."

"Her phone and her clothes," Detective Hatcher remarked. "Now that sounds very familiar."

It was shocking to think that Darby might have masterminded such a ruthless plan to fake her own death. "But why would she have done something so extreme?" I asked. "And how could she have finagled it in the caves?"

"These are great questions," the detective said. "Would she have been trying to run from something? I'll be checking into her financial situation tomorrow, but I understand she'd inherited substantial wealth from her father when he died."

"That's what I was told, as well," I said. "She was letting her stepmother and her new husband live in the family house that she owned. And as for something she'd be running from—that could be her ex-boyfriend, Sterling. He was known to be physically abusive, and he was pushing her to pay off his gambling debts. Didn't her friend Florence call you about that?"

"Not that I've heard of, but we're very short-staffed today." He hesitated. "You're talking about Sterling Caldwell?"

"That's the one—I'm guessing he's the only Sterling around."

Detective Hatcher gave a low whistle. "I'll have to tread carefully when I question him. His mom is Cora Caldwell."

"As in Judge Caldwell?" I asked. Judge Caldwell was well-known in these parts for taking a hard line against criminals. Apparently, she was oblivious to the fact that her own son was involved in an underground gambling club.

"That's the one." The detective groaned. "I'd better get to work. Thank you two for your insights. Let's hope I can get to the bottom of this quickly—but if this actually was a faked death-turned-murder situation, I've got my work cut out for me."

ALTHOUGH IT WAS difficult to drag out of bed on Friday, I was looking forward to spending time with the shelter dogs. It was like a grand adventure, meeting new dogs with differing personalities every time I worked.

When Bo had concocted the idea of starting a cafe in our hometown, he'd had me in mind, since he knew that when I was growing up, I'd considered dogs my best friends. They weren't fickle like most of the teen girls at school. I'd poured out my angsty teen troubles to my canine companions, and they had always seemed to feel my pain. I still did that with Coal, and, like all the dogs I'd owned, he seemed to shoulder my burdens as his own.

But the shelter dogs that came through the cafe had their own burdens. Although Summer dreamed of shifting her shelter into a no-kill facility that focused primarily on pet foster programs, it simply wasn't feasible, given the number of abandoned pets in our area. She would have to turn away numerous "unadoptable" or old animals, leaving them with nowhere else to go. But she worked tirelessly to place her cats and dogs in foster homes, and our cafe had also facilitated many happy dog-human matches, so her shelter had the lowest euthanasia rate in the state.

Still, as I spent time with each dog that came through the Barks section, I seemed to feel the clock ticking on their behalf. I determined to find one good thing about each of them—even the unruly ones—and try to point that out to our cafe customers. Bristol had learned to do the same thing.

Milo was helping Bo open the cafe, but when I greeted him, he merely gave a tired wave. His hair looked a little disheveled, and I wasn't quite sure whether his striped pants matched his plaid shirt.

"You hanging in there?" I asked.

He turned on the dishwasher so it would be ready for action. "Briggs was over last night. He was hysterical. He couldn't believe Darby was dead."

As Bo ran a little fresh-perked coffee through the espresso maker to make sure Wednesday's cleaner had been thoroughly rinsed out, he shot me a knowing look. Last night when we'd split up the leftovers, I'd filled him in on the situation, and he had agreed with Titan and me that it was possible Darby had faked her own death. But we weren't at liberty to share that conjecture, leaving Milo and Briggs completely in the dark as to actual possibilities of what had happened to Darby.

"I'm sorry. Have you heard anything else from Florence? I really hope someone's checking in with her." I couldn't shake the feeling she'd put herself in danger, sharing about Sterling's abuse. Although I'd like to believe justice was blind and didn't play favorites, Judge Caldwell could certainly make Florence's life miserable if she got called in to testify against her son.

Milo got the music going on the speakers. He and Bristol were in charge of choosing trendy, yet relaxing tunes to set the right kind of cafe vibe for us. "Briggs is texting her every day. Though I don't know if that's a good thing—together, they're completely unhinged about the whole thing."

I needed to head back to the Barks section, but all three of the dogs Summer had dropped off earlier were relatively old and slow. They seemed perfectly content to roll around in the patches of sunlight on the mats.

"What about Olivia?" I asked. "How's she reacting, do you know? And Nina and Lamont?"

Milo twisted his lip. "I have no idea about Nina and Lamont, but Olivia's still doing her holistic foods thing. She's coming over to our house this afternoon to coach my mom, actually."

One of the dogs gave a growl, so I headed through the gate to the Barks section. The grizzled older dog was trying to swipe a chew bone from one of the smaller dogs, so I remedied that issue by giving him one of his own. Milo was busy at the coffee bar, so I decided to pick our conversation up at some later time.

The day passed uneventfully until noon, when an older woman with frizzy salt-and-pepper hair and a wooden cane advanced on the coffee bar like she was coming to occupy enemy territory. Her demanding voice carried the faintest hint of a British accent.

"I'm not interested in coffee or finger sandwiches," she announced. "However, I wondered if you might be able to produce a decent spot of tea. The wind's picked up, and I'm nearly frozen." She cast a glance at the fireplace. "Of course it's a gas fire. Heaven forbid we use real logs or have real smoke in a business place!"

Fortunately, Kylie was working the cash register and not Milo, who was actively sneering at the woman from behind the milk jug he was holding. Kylie was an expert at handling fractious customers, because her previous job was working the Dunkin' Donuts drive-through.

"Yes, ma'am, it's turned chilly, hasn't it? I can brew you a fresh cup of Earl Grey—how does that sound? Or would you prefer a London Fog latte?"

"London Fog latte? What sort of atrocity is that? Coffee mixed with tea, I'll imagine. No, indeed. I'll have a plain black tea, with two sweeteners. No funny business."

By this point, I was having trouble hiding my wide grin. It was a good thing Bo was on lunch break, because I had the feeling he would have shut down the woman's impudence in a hurry. But since only a couple of people were in the cafe, and they were wearing headphones and working on laptops, I was getting a kick out of our royal British highness.

After the woman paid—coins jangling as she retrieved them from her wallet—she bypassed the fireplace entirely. Instead, she slowly made her way toward the Barks section.

Was I going to have the pleasure of having her enter my shelter dog fiefdom?

She glanced over the divider wall, then gave a loud "*hmph*" before settling into a chair. Feeling personally affronted—had she decided the Barks section wasn't clean enough?—I stood, washed my hands, and walked out the gate to her small table.

Extending a hand, I said, "Hi. I'm Macy Hatfield, one of the owners of this cafe. How lovely you could drop by today. Are you here on a visit?"

The woman's watery blue eyes roamed over me. "I should think not. I've been a resident of this town for well over a year now. Just because I haven't frequented your startup cafe doesn't mean I'm some sort of an outsider."

My eyes widened, but before I could formulate any kind of retort, Kylie carried the woman's teacup over. "One piping hot cuppa with two sweeteners." She gave me a quick wink as she set the cup on the table.

"Thank you." The woman's words were faint, as if she only tacked on politeness once her demands were fully met.

Recovering my equilibrium, I said, "I hope you enjoy your tea—what was your name, again?"

She frowned, as if everyone in town should know who she was. And quite possibly they did, but for all the wrong reasons. "I'm Matilda Crump. I'm in the garden club, the book club, and the historical society." She ripped into her sweetener packets with gusto.

"Matilda Crump?" I echoed. "I believe you know my neighbor, Vera Cox. I'll be speaking at the book club next month, actually."

Her lips puckered. I suppose it was a bit of sour grapes

to learn that I was connected myself. Not that I had anything to prove—I was born in this area, for Pete's sakes. And Barks & Beans was hardly a startup, since it was quickly becoming one of the most successful businesses in town.

She took a long slurp of her tea, smacking her lips afterward as if sizing up the quality of Kylie's brew.

I lowered my voice. "Am I right in thinking you were the one who found Darby Whitmore's body in that abandoned house?"

Matilda jerked her head my direction. She squinted at me through her thick glasses lenses. "I was. It was shocking." For a moment, she seemed almost flustered. "I've had nightmares every night since. I knew something strange was going on over there—lights on weird hours of the night, and I could've sworn I heard a dog barking in there. I didn't see one, though."

I was actually glad to find that Matilda had been bothered by Darby's death, since I was beginning to wonder if she had any normal human emotions. "What caused you to go into the house?" I asked. Titan had explained the scenario, but I wondered if she had anything to add.

"There was a light on upstairs, you see. It shone out a crack in the boarded-up window into my room. It was late, and I couldn't get to sleep knowing someone was camped out in a condemned house. I went over and knocked on the front door, but no one answered. I tried it, but it was locked. Out of sheer desperation, I went around back and knocked. The door actually swung open, and I wondered if something wasn't wrong."

"So you decided to peep in?" I asked, knowing she'd done a lot more than peep.

"I did." She took another slurp of tea and once again smacked her lips. I tried to hide my cringe as she continued her story. "Normally, I avoid steep stairs, but when I called out and no one answered, I knew in my gut that I needed to check on things."

I had to hand it to her—it must not have been easy getting upstairs with her cane, especially if the rest of the house was dark.

"You didn't have a phone?" I asked.

She stared at me as if I were from another planet. "I don't own a mobile phone, but if I did, I certainly wouldn't tote it about like an extra appendage, the way you youngsters do."

I decided to take that as a roundabout compliment, since she'd lumped me in with the youth. "Did you see anything unusual?"

"Besides a dead girl lying next to an old mattress, do you mean?" She gave me a sharp look, as if suddenly realizing I was asking a lot of questions. A dog whined in the Barks section and I knew my time was up.

But Matilda surprised me with an unexpected morsel of information. "I found something else—a Queen of Hearts playing card, just lying on her chest. I assumed someone must've placed it there after she died."

Neither Detective Hatcher nor Titan had mentioned this detail. I wondered why, but Matilda answered the question for me.

"I thought it was in very poor taste, so I tucked the card into my sweater and took it back home with me."

11

Now it was my turn to stare. "You're saying you didn't turn the card over to the police?" I asked incredulously.

She took a swig of tea, her tone brooking no argument. "It was in very poor taste, as I said. As if someone wanted to mock her for being homeless by saying she was some kind of queen."

"But they'll need to dust it for fingerprints," I said. "Her killer might have handled it. Besides, Darby was incredibly wealthy—haven't you seen that on the news?"

She raised her beaklike nose into the air. "I rarely watch the news."

Were we living in the Dark Ages? Did this woman really think she had some kind of right to abscond with evidence from a murder scene?

The dog whined again, and I softened my tone. "Matilda, I think it would be wise if you turned that card over to the police now. I'll let my friend Detective Hatcher know you have it."

I was leaving her no wiggle room. After mentioning the detective was my friend, she seemed to rethink her position. "Of course. I'll call them once I get home."

"Thank you." I started walking toward the Barks section, but turned to add, "And thank you for dropping in." Despite her snooty ways and complete ignorance of police procedure, Matilda had brought to light a new piece of evidence.

And that evidence seemed to point all the more strongly to Sterling Caldwell, the gambler who didn't know when to hold 'em...much less when to walk away.

TITAN CAME to my house after work. I shared about Matilda while we played with Coal in the garden, and he was just as appalled as I had been about her sneaking off with that playing card.

Once Coal was resting inside, I suggested we hit our favorite Mexican restaurant, since I was already feeling hungry.

It turned out the place was almost empty this time of day, so our food was brought to the table quickly. As I methodically dipped my chicken quesadilla wedge into guacamole, salsa, and sour cream, Titan suggested we look around downtown Lewisburg. "I feel like I'm always here, but I rarely get to slow down and enjoy things," he said. "What would you recommend?"

I knew Titan wasn't a big shopper, so the antique stores might bore him. Without thinking things through, I suggested, "Do you like artwork?"

"Sure do," he said.

Only after I'd spoken did it hit me that the owner of

The Discerning Palette art gallery was Dylan Butler, a handsome guy I'd dated several times when I'd come back to town. I'd since explained to Dylan that I now had a boyfriend, but I hadn't exactly explained to Titan about Dylan. Trying to backtrack, I said, "Actually, the art gallery might be closing soon."

He glanced at his phone. "It's only a quarter after five. Surely they stay open until six?"

I felt trapped. My palms actually started sweating, which was something I thought only happened in books. "Oh, sure. Yeah, I guess so." I shoved my drink straw into my mouth, taking a long sip of sweet tea to shut myself up.

"Sounds great." Titan assembled a perfectly proportioned bite of steak, rice, and pico de gallo on his fork. "Tell me about your conversation with Matilda again—do you really believe she was so clueless as to pocket evidence from a crime scene without any thought of possible repercussions?"

THE DISCERNING PALETTE was relatively empty when we entered. I could see at a glance that Dylan was still showcasing the unusual portraits from a younger artist he'd stumbled onto during a trip to Washington, D.C. They drew the eye faster than anything else in the shop.

Dylan's assistant, Shanda, walked over to greet us. The perky woman was in her early sixties, and she seemed to genuinely like everyone who entered the store. "How delightful to see you today, Macy. How's the cafe? I can't get over that lavender honey latte you make. I could drink that stuff out of a vat." She glanced at Titan, then gave me a sly grin. "And who is this fine young man you've brought along today?"

"Titan McCoy," I said. I wanted to ask if Dylan was around so I could be prepared, but I didn't want to make a big deal out of the fact I knew him.

But Dylan's voice preceded him. "Titan. I've heard a lot about you." The art gallery owner strode out of the back room, and I had the sudden urge to dash out the glass entry doors. Of course, he looked just as Cary Grant as ever with his cleft chin, dapper blazer, and dark blue button-up that matched his eyes.

Titan extended a hand. Although Dylan had once told me he was six feet tall, he looked almost short compared to Titan's muscled six-foot-five frame. How he'd "heard a lot about" Titan was beyond me, since I certainly hadn't told him anything about my new boyfriend. Maybe Bo had chatted with him about Titan, though, since Dylan had helped him choose artwork for the cafe and they were still good friends.

Dylan didn't look especially cowed by Titan, which was a relief. I didn't want him throwing off the kind of macho vibes Titan would definitely pick up on. But Dylan did hold my hand a second too long when he welcomed me. "Macy—long time, no see," he said.

His eyes met mine, and I felt like a heel. Why on earth had I suggested parading my boyfriend into his shop? It seemed almost like a subconscious thing.

"I see you're still selling paintings from your portrait artist." I hoped I sounded like a casual friend, just a supporter of the arts in this town.

Dylan warmed to one of his favorite topics. "I can't believe how many I've sold. Jameson can't crank them out fast enough to keep up with demand. I'm selling them online now, too."

"That's wonderful," I murmured. "We'll just walk around and check things out."

Dylan smiled. "Nice to meet you, Titan. Take good care of her." He headed toward a back room, and Shanda sat down at the main desk.

As we rounded a corner into a section highlighting local landscape artists, Titan glanced down at me. "You guys are friends?" he asked quietly.

"Just friends." My tone was firm. "I did date him a little when I moved back, but that all ended with you."

Before I had a chance to explain further, the door opened and Hudson Donovan walked in. The blond was wearing a gray V-neck pullover with a crown featured in the middle of it, which somehow seemed apt. He grinned when he saw me.

"If it isn't Macy Hatfield. How's my brother been doing? I hardly see him, since we basically keep different hours. I hope his work hasn't slacked off—he and his friends are taking poor Darby's demise quite hard, I'm afraid."

He seemed very cavalier about Darby's death, which was undoubtedly a murder. Unsure how to respond, I assured him that Milo was working as hard as ever, then I introduced him to Titan.

Hudson pointed to one of the black and white portraits of a woman with an elongated neck and arms. She was holding a beat-up backpack and looked as if she were homeless, but her face was practically glowing like an angel. "I'm buying one of Jameson's portraits," he said. "It's titled *Street Siren*."

"It's gorgeous," I said, wishing I could afford one.

As Titan wandered over to look at the portrait gallery, Hudson leaned in. "As a matter of fact, we're going to be having a memorial meeting of our gambling club later on tonight, in honor of Darby. I'd love it if you could join us."

He was asking me to a meeting of the secret club Darby had been involved in? I couldn't imagine why he'd assume I could gamble with the heavy-hitters. Maybe he thought the Barks & Beans Cafe was raking in the dough. While it was true that I wasn't poor, I also didn't have money to blow on poker—nor would I even want to. "I'm not a gambler," I said.

"There's no obligation to participate." His voice was smooth, and, like Daisy Buchanan in *The Great Gatsby*, it was full of money. I could almost close my eyes and envision tranquil days on deep blue waters, eating crudités on a yacht.

I supposed it couldn't hurt to get an insider view of the world Darby had moved in. Maybe I'd discover something helpful to share with Detective Hatcher. "Uh, okay—I guess so."

Hudson straightened and gave a brisk nod, as if I'd made the right choice. "It's at my place at nine. Milo can fill you in on the details. Just so you know, we call ourselves The Barons." He winked and walked toward the back, where Dylan was talking with Shanda by the computer.

Titan made his way back to my side. It was almost as if he'd sensed that Hudson wanted to discuss something Darby-related with me. As we headed back to the car, I explained that I'd be going over to Hudson's place tonight for a memorial gambling event, which admittedly sounded completely bizarre. But Titan didn't ask any questions, which I appreciated, because I was pretty sure Hudson's invite didn't extend to him.

"Be careful," he warned. "Stick close to Milo and watch out for Sterling, if he shows up. Even though it's entirely possible Nina and Lamont cooked up a scheme to get rid of Darby, it could also have been one of her so-called 'friends.'"

AFTER TITAN DROPPED me off and headed back to his cabin, I tried to determine if I had anything appropriate to wear to a gambling party with The Barons. I was about to text Milo for help with the task when Detective Hatcher called me.

"The witness who discovered Darby's body just called me, saying she'd forgotten to give me something. She said you'd recommended she contact me. Do you know anything about this? I'm on my way to pick it up at her house."

I laid out the unbelievable story of how Matilda had decided to snatch the playing card, and the detective blew out a long breath. "She did sound rather flustered. I wasn't sure what to make of it. Here's hoping she didn't destroy any prints. I'd better go—I'm nearly to her house. Thanks, Macy."

Surprisingly, I felt a little bad for Matilda. She didn't have any reasonable explanation as to why she'd taken a playing card from a dead woman's chest. Although Charlie Hatcher was courteous, he also wasn't the kind of detective who would turn a blind eye to the fact that the older lady had knowingly swiped evidence.

After thumbing through clothes in my closet, I finally gave up and called Milo. To my surprise, he sounded a bit irritated that I was coming to his brother's place tonight, but he instructed me to wear the same thing I'd worn to our adoption party for Charity's grandson, which was a white shirt, jeans, and a navy cardigan. I was surprised he'd remembered my outfit that day, but, like Bristol, he did have a good eye for detail.

"Where does Hudson live?" I asked.

"He's next door to our main house, in a renovated stable." He gave me the address. "Listen, you need to be careful around that crowd." He sighed. "I wasn't planning on showing up, but now I know you're going to be there, I'll meet you at the front door at nine."

Things felt topsy-turvy, as if my young barista were attempting to protect his thirty-eight-year-old boss, but I didn't want to turn up my nose at his offer. "That would be great. Thank you, Milo." I hesitated. "You don't gamble, do you?"

"I work hard for my money, so no, I don't. Briggs, however, has spent a lot of time researching how to get good at poker, and I have to admit he's done fairly well for himself. He'll be there tonight, too."

"Okay. I'm not gambling either, so hopefully I won't stick out like a sore thumb. I'll see you there."

Coal had positioned himself on his pillow, but seemed to be listening to my conversation. As I pulled out the outfit Milo had recommended I wear, Coal gave a long whine.

"I'm sorry to leave you alone tonight," I said. "What do you want to watch? *Knight Rider*? *Fixer Upper*?" I left the TV on when I had to go places at night, so Coal wouldn't feel so lonely, and those were two of his favorite shows. When he gave a small yowl of response, I said, "*Fixer Upper* it is."

As I added a long necklace, I explained to Coal what I

was doing. He looked at me intently, as if he wasn't quite sure of my plan to infiltrate The Barons, but when I tossed him a doggie treat, he acted a little more enthusiastic.

By the time I headed out the door and locked up, Coal was settled onto the couch, watching TV. It almost felt like I was leaving an older child at home by himself. Of course, I didn't have children, but I imagined they were far more worrisome than a Great Dane with separation anxiety.

I gave Bo a quick call from the car, letting him know what I was up to. Sometimes he went for runs at night, and he paid attention to whether I was home or not. That was the kind of big brother thing he did, and I really didn't mind. In fact, I felt a bit adrift during the rare times he was out of town. But Vera always picked up the slack, checking in with me because she knew I didn't like to be alone. Maybe I had separation anxiety, too.

When I pulled into the open gates at the end of the Donovans' driveway, I gave a small squeal of surprise. I'd expected a large, modern home, but Milo's family had updated an older brick two-story house, then very tastefully added onto it. A proper southern porch wrapped around the front.

A matching building sat next to the main house. When Milo had said his brother lived in a renovated stable, I certainly hadn't pictured a two-story that was a house in and of itself. Established hedges and trees had been optimally positioned around both houses.

Although I was a little early, another car pulled in behind me, so I parked and got out. Briggs hopped out of his BMW and jaunted over to me.

"Nice to see you," he said. "Milo invite you?"

"Actually, Hudson did." We stood outside the wooden front door, waiting for Milo to meet us.

Briggs kicked at the pea gravel. "I don't know what possessed Hudson to throw a memorial party like this, but I decided I shouldn't miss it. Still, it seems kind of gauche."

As we lingered by the door, someone pulled up in a shiny blue Tesla. Sterling eased out of the driver's seat, then strode around to open the passenger door for Olivia.

As the brunette super-couple stalked by us, Sterling said hello. Olivia continued looking straight ahead, as if Briggs and I were mere bugs.

"She doesn't like me," Briggs said, loud enough for anyone to hear.

Milo was walking our way from the main house. "You're just now figuring it out, bro?" He clapped Briggs on the back, then crooked an elbow and extended it toward me. "Care to join us for an evening of lackluster entertainment, my lady?" he joked.

I linked my arm through his. If nothing else, at least I'd get to know my very private upper-class employee a little better tonight. "I'd be happy to," I said.

12

I really shouldn't have been surprised that the interior of Hudson's place was just as swanky as the exterior, but I was. The place had been immaculately decorated, with name-brand logos showing up on pillows, wallpaper, and more.

Hudson came out to greet us. He gave me a European-style greeting, air-kissing each cheek. "So glad you could come to honor Darby's memory with us," he said. "Let me show you to the library."

I wasn't sure why we needed to see the library, but once he turned the corner into the expansive room, I understood. Apparently, this was where they gambled, since a large table neatly arranged with poker chips and stacks of cards dominated the center of the room.

I glanced around, marveling at the book collections lining the shelves. "Would you mind if I checked out the bookcases really quickly?" I asked Milo, extricating my arm from his.

"No, you go ahead. I should've guessed you're the

bookish type," he said. "I'm heading into the bar for some snacks—it's the next room over."

Briggs broke off from us to speak with Florence, who was basically hiding in a tall wingback chair in the corner. She seemed to be undergoing a transformation since Darby's death, and I didn't feel it was healthy. She'd been far more confident when she was hanging out with her girl-pack leader friend. Now she almost seemed to be shrinking into herself.

I glanced around for Olivia to see if she'd noticed Florence's loneliness, but I should've known she'd be oblivious. She was sipping on a glass of champagne, chatting it up with Sterling and another couple.

Making my way around the bookshelf perimeter, I chuckled to see Hudson's book choices. While he had a few leather-bound classics on the shelves, he also had the entire Hardy Boys series, the *Hunger Games* trilogy, and a big pile of old video game magazines. I was beginning to get a more complete picture of who Hudson was.

I halted when I caught sight of a framed photo that had been tucked behind a red racecar model. In the picture, Hudson looked maybe five years younger, and his arm was draped around Darby. They wore swimsuits and were sitting on a yacht, and they looked unabashedly in love.

This was not something Milo had mentioned to me.

I jumped when Hudson spoke quietly behind me. "The golden years of our youth," he said wistfully. "As you can see, Darby and I were close once. I've tried to put that era behind me. She decided to chase after Sterling instead."

Unsure how to respond, I murmured, "I'm sorry for your loss."

He shrugged. "Like I said, it's in the past." Leaning in, he asked, "Are you ready for a little fun tonight?"

I got the distinct feeling he was flirting with me, but I must be ten years older than him. Reading the confused look on my face, he added, "I meant do you want to throw a little money in the pot? We're not playing for high stakes tonight, so everyone can participate."

Not flirting then. "Oh, no. I just came to watch. I take it you're the head honcho? The game-master or whatever you call it?"

He smiled. "Actually, our real head honcho is a woman. I haven't even met her. She contacted me out of the blue, said she'd heard I was a bit of a card shark, and wondered if I'd like to start an exclusive gambling club in this area. It's not strictly *legal* with the kind of stakes we use, so we keep it secret."

"Does she keep a cut?" I knew that was definitely against the law.

His pupils darkened. "You're getting awfully curious, Macy. And you know what they say about curiosity and the cat."

On the heels of that thinly veiled threat, Hudson brightened and turned to face the room. He clapped his hands together and said, "Welcome, everyone. I'm sure you've had enough time to get a little refreshment. As you know, the reason we're here is to honor Darby. She was one of us, and we feel her loss in the depths of our souls. She would want us to go on living our lives, though, so how about all you gamblers gather at the table so we can get started."

It felt a little surreal to see Darby's friends hustling over to play poker in her honor, but to each his own, I supposed.

Milo was nowhere in sight, so I guessed he was still snacking at the bar.

Florence had stayed put in her turquoise wingback chair, so I headed into the corner to talk with her. Maybe she could give me information on Darby's failed relationships.

"Hi." I eased into a nearby chintz armchair. "You don't gamble?"

"Sometimes, but I didn't feel like it tonight," she said.

"I understand. I just came to pay my respects."

We sat in silence for a few minutes. When the conversation at the gambling table grew louder, I said, "I just found out that Darby and Hudson dated years ago. Since she was part of the gambling club, I'm assuming they got along okay nowadays?"

Florence nodded. "It was an amiable breakup, from what Darby told me. She said they just didn't have the right chemistry."

From the looks of the photo, they'd had plenty of chemistry, but I didn't point that out. "And her breakup with Sterling was...less than amiable, I'm guessing?"

She darted a quick look at the table, where Sterling was moving chips around. "Definitely not friendly."

"Milo said you'd told Briggs you saw Sterling hit Darby—did that happen a lot?"

She gave a quick nod. "He gets stupid drunk sometimes, especially when he gambles. One time I thought he was going to hit me."

"And Olivia knows this? Why is she with him now?"

Florence shifted the cheese and crackers on her plate, making flower designs with them. It didn't look like she'd touched her food. "I don't know." She set her plate down on the side table, watching the poker game for a few moments. Then she turned to me. "Actually, to be honest, I don't think Olivia likes me much. When I told her, she accused me of wanting Sterling for myself."

Wow, the girl drama just never ended with this group. "That's ridiculous," I said.

"Olivia's always wanted to be in charge of our group of friends," Florence said. "She felt like I was somehow a threat to her, since I was closer to Darby. She was always trying to take me down a peg by telling lies about me."

I watched Olivia as she laughed at the table and patted Sterling's hand. It was clear she enjoyed being a social butterfly.

Milo finally came our way, a loaded plate of appetizers in hand. After settling in a chair next to me, he held out his plate. "Care for a chicken wing, or maybe a barbeque meatball?"

I was feeling a little hungry, but I didn't want to take Milo's food. "Thank you, but I'll grab a plate for myself." I stood and walked toward the doorway he'd emerged from.

The bar room was lovely, with textured wallpaper and leather bar stools. Briggs was sitting in one of them, sipping from a can of Coke.

"Macy," he said warmly. Patting the bar stool next to him, he said, "Please have a seat. I needed a caffeine break so I could get back on my A-game."

"Oh, sure. Just a sec." I filled a small plate and grabbed a water bottle from the mini-fridge. It took some effort for me to climb into the high stool, which seemed to have been designed for tall people, but I finally succeeded. "This is quite a place, isn't it?"

Briggs gave a forlorn nod, then, to my dismay, his eyes

welled with tears. I had the sinking feeling he might start crying, and I had no idea what to say to stop it.

Running a hand through his dark hair, he said, "She's dead. She's really dead." His desperate eyes met mine. "And someone *killed* her, they said. It's a homicide. I can't understand."

"You really cared for her deeply, didn't you?" I asked, hoping to take his mind off the murder aspect.

"I did. I really did. More than anyone else. More than her loser ex-boyfriend, Sterling, that's for sure. He doesn't care about anyone but himself." Briggs took another fortifying sip of Coke and continued. "To be honest, I loved her. I've loved her for years—since we were kids." He was getting worked up. "Am I not attractive enough? Is that what's wrong with me?"

I wasn't quite sure what he wanted me to say, but I murmured, "Of course you're attractive. Maybe she could only see you as a friend since you'd known each other so long. Maybe in time, she would've returned your feelings." I was basically grasping at straws, but hopefully something I said would comfort him.

"I wrote songs for her," he said wistfully. "I sent them to her, and I sang them with my band. She never said a thing about them. Maybe I should've come right out and told her I loved her. Now I'll never get that chance."

He drained his pop can and dropped it into the stainless steel recycling bin nearby. He looked like a dejected kid who'd just lost his favorite toy. "I guess I'll go back to the table," he said, as if waiting for guidance.

When I didn't say anything, he plodded off. Olivia swept into the bar, setting her empty glass on the counter and daintily filling a plate.

"How are you?" I was genuinely curious to know if she was taking Darby's death as lightly as it seemed.

Her answer came fast and smooth. "I'm good." Her dazzling white smile took me by surprise, since she'd basically ignored me on her way into the house. "And how are you? It's hard to believe everything that's happened since that terrible day in the caverns."

"I'm doing okay." I leaned on the counter, giving her the side-eye. "I don't know about you, but I think it's pretty worrisome they found her in that house. It seems odd."

Olivia took a drink of her sparkling water, then adeptly situated herself on the stool next to me. She was tall, so the stool height wasn't an issue for her. "Oh, I agree. It's so strange. Why was she in that random house? Was she into meth or something?"

That was an unusual take, but empty buildings *were* sometimes used to cook crystal meth around these parts. "I don't think they've found anything pointing to that," I said cautiously. "Don't you think you would've known if she'd been into drugs?"

Olivia gave an elegant shrug. "They say it's hard to tell." She glanced toward the gambling table, where the players were getting louder. "I'd better get back to Sterling—he's such a go-getter."

As she stood, my deep-seated motherly instincts took over, and I gave her loose sleeve a tug. "Olivia, you *are* aware that Darby told people Sterling physically abused her, right? I'm confused as to why you'd be dating him if you knew that."

She leveled a fierce glare on me. "How dare you insinuate that? That's just gossip—probably spread by Florence. She's just bitter that Sterling went for me instead of her."

She marched out of the bar, her high heels jabbing into the carpet.

I munched in silence on my pickles and olives, observing the gambling table. Briggs was yelling at Hudson, who looked exasperated. Sterling was thumbing through his cards, impatiently tapping his foot. Olivia had sat down next to him, and she proceeded to cup her hand and whisper something in his ear.

My gaze drifted toward Milo and Florence. Neither of them had budged from their chairs, and they looked equally bored. I wasn't sure why Milo was sticking around, since I was a big girl who could take care of myself, but maybe he was running interference for his moody friend Briggs.

I carried my empty water bottle over to the recycling bin, looking for the slot for plastics. I might as well head home, since I wasn't even gambling. I'd managed to talk to everyone I'd wanted to.

I'd just dropped my bottle in when a low, growly voice sounded close to my ear. "Trying to clean up your mess?"

I turned quickly, only to see Sterling was looming behind me. Although his good looks were literally breath-taking—tall, dark, and handsome—his eyes were bleary, and I could smell alcohol on his breath.

"I'm no abuser," he said. In direct contradiction to his words, he started backing me toward the wall. "Don't go telling lies on me to my girlfriend. Darby always was a liar, and so's her little friend, Florence. You can't believe a word they say." His breath was hot on my face, and I couldn't shrink back any more.

Suddenly I wondered why I was cowering at all. I was in a house I'd been invited to, and I was being accosted by a drunken guest. I had every right to defend myself. I could almost hear Bo's voice in my head saying, "Hit him where it hurts."

I was about to do just that when Milo's golden head appeared in the room. In a leisurely tone, he said, "Now, now, Sterling. Let's not make a scene. You know Hudson'll kick you out of The Barons if you do something stupid."

Sterling blinked, as if coming to his senses. Very slowly, he wagged his finger back and forth in my face. "No more lies," he ordered, then abruptly turned and stormed from the room.

Milo immediately walked over to my side and wrapped a steadying arm around me. His nonchalant demeanor evaporated as concern filled his eyes. "Are you okay? I can't believe he thought he could threaten you here. I don't know what would've happened if I hadn't interrupted him."

While I wasn't sure what Sterling would've done, I'd been ready with my next step, which was to knee him in the groin and send him writhing to the ground in pain. But I was grateful Milo had stepped in, so things didn't have to escalate. I didn't want to lose the rapport I had with his brother, who seemed to be a valuable connection to have.

One thing was certain after Sterling's disturbing behavior tonight—it wasn't a stretch to believe he could've physically intimidated and harmed Darby. But would he have poisoned her in cold blood? That seemed like more of a calculated move, and Sterling seemed far more head-strong than strategic.

I was ready to leave the darkened bar and the strained group dynamics of The Barons. All I wanted was to curl up in pajamas with a good book and Coal at the foot of my bed. I gave Milo's arm a squeeze. "Thank you for coming to my rescue. I won't forget it. I'm going to head home—this really isn't my kind of scene."

But as I walked into the library, I soon realized it wasn't going to be as easy to leave as I'd hoped.

Nina Styles stood in the doorway, hands on her hips. She was wearing yoga pants, a tie-dyed hoodie, and bright orange tennis shoes. Her angry eyes roved around the room until they landed on Florence, then she charged straight for her.

13

As Nina advanced on Florence, she kept clenching her outstretched hands. It actually looked like she was going to strangle her, so I hurried over and stepped into the space between them. Holding out a hand of warning, I said, "Is there something you wanted?"

Hudson was by my side in an instant. Although he projected a calm persona like his brother, I could practically feel the waves of indignation emanating from his tense body. "Nina, why are you in my house? In my *library*?" he demanded.

She turned a scathing look on him. "Don't think I'm not aware of your little poker parties over here. Darby told us about them. But I didn't come to talk about that. I came to ask Florence what made her think she could get away with this."

Florence looked utterly confused. Her legs wobbled as she stood to face Nina, so I placed a bracing arm around her. "Get away with what?" she asked.

Nina's dirty looks only intensified. "You're getting Darby's house and most of her money. How did you finagle that? We're her family!"

Florence gasped. "I didn't know about this. What are you talking about? She didn't leave me anything."

By this point, everyone had gathered around Florence's wingback chair. Both Sterling and Olivia looked every bit as dumbfounded as Florence. Briggs acted a bit hurt, though he wouldn't have had reason to think Darby left him anything.

Nina scoffed, "Don't play innocent with me, girlie. You were always over at the house, thick as thieves with my daughter. Now she's gone, and you're inheriting a fortune! You must've poisoned her against us!"

Strange that Nina should choose the word "poisoned." I tried to size her up as she stood there, bold as brass in someone else's house. Obviously, she'd expected Darby's fortune—and her house—to fall to her. Had she been desperate enough to kill her stepdaughter, thinking she'd be the one to inherit?

Briggs, who'd apparently recovered his composure, jumped into the fray. "Nina, let's not forget that you're only Darby's *step*mother. You aren't related by blood. She had no obligation to continue supporting you financially, like she has since her dad died. Do you even have a job?"

The line of rage had definitely been crossed. Nina practically screamed, "I don't have to listen to this! I'm talking with our lawyer and we're going to try and get that will revoked!" She pointed a manicured burgundy fingernail at Florence. "You're not going to win, you grasping cow!"

Milo and Briggs moved in, each taking one of Nina's

arms and forcing her out of the library. Hudson straightened his shirt and took a deep breath. He placed a hand on Florence's shoulder. "I'm so sorry about that. Are you okay?"

Florence looked dazed. "I can't—I don't know what's going on," she said. "As far as I knew, Darby was leaving everything to Nina. Not Lamont, because she said she didn't trust him, but she'd always said her dad would've wanted her to look out for Nina. He had married her, after all. That was why she let Nina stay on at the house."

I had wondered why Darby had allowed her stepmother and Lamont to stick around, but it must've been out of a sense of obligation to her dead father's wishes. It would be logical that she'd leave her money to Nina, then.

Olivia gave a superior sniff. "What I'd like to know is why that woman is looking into the will so soon anyway."

Hudson's answer was swift. "Because she needs the money. It's common knowledge that she already ran through the money Darby's dad left her. Plus, she'll have Darby's burial expenses coming up, and she probably wants to know if she's going to wind up homeless in the process."

Briggs and Milo returned to the library. "We locked the door," Milo said. "She won't be making a return appearance. Someone must've left it unlocked."

"Thanks, bro." Hudson dusted his hands together, as if done with the inconveniences of the evening. "Let's get back to poker, shall we?"

Sterling and Olivia walked toward the table. Briggs asked Florence if she was okay, and she assured him she was, so he headed back to finish the game.

But I could tell Florence was not even vaguely okay. She

gave an occasional tremble, and chill bumps ran up both her arms.

"I can run you home," I said. "I'm sure Hudson wouldn't mind if you left your car here for awhile. Or maybe Milo or Briggs could drop it off at your place."

She seemed to consider my suggestion. "I'll need my car for work tomorrow," she finally said. "But I really don't feel like driving. Could you ask Briggs if he'd mind dropping it off in front of my house? He knows where I live." She fished her keyless car remote out of her purse and handed it to me.

"Of course," I said. "You can wait for me in the entryway. I'll be right there."

BRIGGS SAID he'd be happy to take Florence's car home, though Milo joked that he'd get dog hair all over his pants. "She takes that dog everywhere," Milo said.

Florence had mentioned she was a dog lover. I wondered if she'd thought about getting a companion dog for the one she had. I grinned as I walked back to the entryway. I was like some kind of busybody matchmaker when it came to placing shelter dogs.

Florence was standing with her hands folded behind her back, staring out the window as if lost in thought.

"You ready?" I asked. "Briggs will bring your car home later tonight."

"Sure." She trailed after me to my vehicle. Once we were situated, she said, "I can't wrap my head around what Nina said. She has to be mistaken. Darby wouldn't have left her house and money to me."

"Maybe she didn't feel she could trust anyone else," I said.

"I know she trusted Briggs, at the very least. Olivia is a flake, but she's not disloyal, either."

Then again, neither Briggs nor Olivia really *needed* Darby's fortune. Maybe that was the reason she left things to Florence. Although Nina was needy, Darby might have decided her obligation to care for her dad's second wife ended with her own death.

She suddenly asked me, "Did you have a good night? I saw Sterling go into the bar...I hoped he was nice to you."

I flicked my eyes her way. "Actually, he wasn't. He was about to corner me when Milo walked in. I'm pretty sure he was drunk."

Florence's tone grew more forceful. "I'm so sorry. That's just like him, cornering people like some kind of wild animal."

I had a flash of insight. "Did he—did he ever corner *you*, Florence?"

She dipped her head, red curls draping her face so I couldn't see her eyes. "A couple of times, when Darby was out of the room. He warned me that I needed to push Darby to give him money. She had plenty of it, he said."

"That's horrible. Did he ever hit you?"

"No, but I knew full well he wanted to. He always seemed so angry."

A new possibility occurred to me. If Sterling had known Darby was going to the caverns that day, he might have plotted a way to attack her. He could've had someone hit the lights, then tried to shove her over in the dark. Somehow she had survived, maybe crawling out through the stream and walking to the abandoned house before anyone saw her. Pretending to be dead would've gotten her out of Sterling's clutches forever. The only thing that didn't quite fit was if he wanted to kill her for her money...maybe when they were dating, she'd told him he was in her will? Then maybe she'd changed it after they broke up?

"You said you didn't see anyone with a baseball cap on in the caves that day?" I asked.

She shook her head. "No, it was just Olivia ahead of us and you all behind."

As I pulled into Florence's driveway, a black van eased in behind us. She turned around, then her eyes widened. "That's Lamont's van. He does handyman jobs for a living."

"Why would he be following us?" I asked.

"Nina was really upset about the will." Florence nervously played with the strap on her purse. "Lamont used to be a bouncer at a club. Maybe she sent him to scare me."

"Not on my watch," I said firmly, pulling my pepper spray from my purse and sticking it in my pocket. "You stay in the car."

I opened my car door and stood up to face him. The sun was setting behind his head, so I couldn't make out his eyes, but he certainly was a stocky guy.

"Could we help you?" I asked loudly, hoping the neighbors might hear me and look out their windows.

As Lamont lumbered toward me, Florence's dog started barking from inside the house. It sounded like it was on the big side—maybe I should've instructed Florence to run in and let her dog out, but it was too late for that. I needed to handle Lamont Styles right here and right now.

"What do you want?" I asked, hand on my pepper spray.

"Nina wanted me to talk with Florence," he said.

"You can talk to me instead. You shouldn't be in her driveway," I said. "She could report you to the police for harassment." I wasn't sure if this was actually true, but it sounded believable.

He got closer, and I was shocked to see a pleading look on his face. "Would you tell Florence that Nina wanted to apologize for her outburst. She lost her head when Darby's lawyer told us about the will, that's all. She hopes she can still be friends."

I almost laughed in his face. Friends? I doubted that. In fact, I could guess why Nina was suddenly trying to gloss over her irate behavior—she hoped Florence would let her keep the house. "I'll tell her," I said.

He leaned down, glancing into my car window. I worried he might go around and try to talk with Florence, but instead, he went back to his van and backed out of the driveway.

Florence's dog was still barking nonstop. Once Lamont was out of sight, I opened the car door and sat down next to her. "Did you hear him?" I asked.

"I did. That was weird."

"I think Nina is trying to catch more flies with honey than with vinegar, like my Auntie A used to say. In other words, she wants something from you."

Florence gave a slow nod. "The house."

"That was my first thought, too. They don't want to be thrown out on their ears, I suppose."

"They've never made any effort to be kind to me, but I suppose I should consider it," she said.

Returning to my theory that Sterling might've tried to

kill Darby, I asked, "Did Sterling know that cashier who worked at the caverns, by any chance?"

"Gabe? Oh, sure. He went to school with us. His name is Gabe Fink, so Sterling and his friends used to call him a rat-fink. He was a bully to him."

That blew a hole in my idea, then. It wouldn't make sense for Gabe to do a favor for Sterling, like hitting the cave lights. If anything, he would've been the first to report it if he'd seen him the day Darby vanished.

Florence shifted in her seat. "I'd better get inside. My dog, Chewie, gets nuts if I leave him alone too long. I named him after Chewbacca in *Star Wars*, but his nickname fits perfectly, since he still chews things up, even at three years old."

Coal wasn't the biggest chewer, and I was grateful for that. "Maybe Chewie's bored and needs a friend," I suggested.

She smiled. "A shelter dog, perhaps? You really are a good marketer for the cafe. I'll think about it." She cast a quick glance behind us, probably to make sure Lamont wasn't lurking somewhere, then got out of the car and hurried up to her front door. The moment she unlocked it, Chewie came bounding into the front yard. He was some kind of a Rottweiler mix, and his chest width was impressive.

Florence came jogging out after him. As I started to back out, he raced toward my car door and leapt up, placing his large paws on my window.

"Chewie, get down!" She shouted, grabbing his collar.

The neon blue collar reminded me of something, but I couldn't think why. Once Florence walked Chewie up to the front porch and had him sit, I backed all the way out into the cul-de-sac. Milo's silver Porsche and a small green car pulled into Florence's drive, so I sat a moment to greet the guys.

Briggs honked the horn of the green car, which must belong to Florence. He was probably reluctant to get out with Florence's big dog around.

And for good reason, since Chewie began growling and lunging, even though Florence held his collar. She quickly walked him into the house, then came out to retrieve her car key fob from Briggs.

They talked for a moment, then Briggs walked around to Milo's passenger seat. Milo backed up next to me and waved. "You hanging out here for some reason?" he asked.

"I just brought Florence home, but I didn't expect you all would clear out so early," I said. "I thought you were sticking around until the end of the poker game, Briggs."

Briggs leaned across the seat to see me better. "I didn't feel like it anymore. It was supposed to be some kind of memorial night for Darby, and instead, it turned into a regular circus when Nina crashed in. Then Sterling and Olivia starting pouting because Darby hadn't left them any money. I'm over it."

Milo looked at me. "I'm sorry it was such a bad experience for you, but I did warn you to be careful around that crowd. I'm glad you left when you did. Sterling gets worse and worse as the night goes on."

"Well, thanks again for intervening on my behalf in the bar," I said. "Y'all get on home. I'm heading back myself."

Milo revved his engine and tore out like he was in a drag race, reminding me of a teen boy. I glanced at Florence's house again to make sure she was safe inside. But she was parking her car in the garage.

I took another look at the back of the small car and felt a jolt of recognition.

The tiny green car. The bright blue dog collar. The dog with the deep barks. I'd seen them all before, and suddenly, I knew where.

Parked on the street outside the abandoned house—on the day Darby vanished from the caverns.

14

As she closed her garage door, Florence noticed I was still sitting in my car. She walked closer. "What's up? Everything okay?" she asked.

It wouldn't hurt to ask her about it. After all, I was sitting safely inside my locked car. Maybe I was jumping to the wrong conclusions.

"I was just thinking I'd seen your car before, when I went walking on a street near the cafe." I watched her face to see if she flinched. "Were you over that way recently—besides the day you came to the cafe, I mean?"

She answered quickly. "No—just that day I visited the dogs at your cafe." She looked like she had no idea what I was talking about.

Maybe I was completely off base and it hadn't been the same car and dog.

"Oh, okay. I was probably mistaken." I turned on my engine. "Sorry for nosing around. Hope you have a great night."

She hesitated. "Listen, Sterling once gave me something

that I haven't told anyone about. I'm wondering if I should report it to the police, or if it's even important. Can you hang on a sec? You can pull up my drive and I'll get your opinion on it, if you don't mind."

Once again, everything circled around to Sterling. "Of course." As she walked toward her door, I pulled up close to the garage and waited.

My phone rang, so I looked at the screen. Hudson Donovan was calling me.

Unsure what else Milo's brother would need to say to me, I picked up.

"Macy," he said. "I'm sorry to bother you. First of all, I wanted to apologize for the scene Nina made tonight." He cleared his throat. "And secondly, Milo told me how abominably Sterling treated you. I cannot believe he thought he could act that way under my roof. I wanted to tell you personally that I'm kicking him out of The Barons. Also, I'm extending an invitation that you can visit our club anytime you want. We meet every other Friday."

"Thanks." I couldn't bring myself to tell him I had no intention of making a repeat visit.

"Also, I had something I wanted to ask you about."

Florence was opening her front door. Anxious to see what Sterling had given her, I said, "Actually, I'm still at Florence's now, but I'll be heading home in a few minutes. Could I call you back then?"

"Sure," he said.

As we said goodbye, I looked over to see Florence coming my way. She had Chewie on a leash, and she was toting an object wrapped in a scarf so bright, it might've come straight out of the Eighties.

"I had to bring him out," she explained. "He needs to go

potty—you know how dogs are." She walked toward my window and extended the object, so I opened the door to look at it.

The moment I swiveled in my seat and placed both feet on the ground, Chewie turned ferocious. He strained at his leash, jumping up and pinning my lap with his paws. Although he wasn't heavier than Coal, all his weight was in the front, so I felt like I couldn't move. Plus, he was baring his teeth.

Instead of reprimanding her dog and yanking him off me, Florence ordered, "Scoot over."

I gave her a confused look. Was this some technique to get him off me? I had a console in the middle of my front seats, so "scooting" wasn't an easy task.

She let out more of Chewie's leash, and, to my horror, he edged further onto my lap. "I'm not kidding." Her voice was unusually gruff.

"I would, but I can't move." I looked at Chewie, who gave a growl.

Florence hesitated a moment. "Okay, I'll pull him off you, but no funny business." She tugged at his leash and said, "Back up." He took a moment to think, then he sat back on his haunches and glared at me.

"Lovely dog," I said, my voice dripping with sarcasm. "I'm going to switch seats now, so keep your beast secure."

Trying to move as quickly as possible, I clambered into the passenger's seat. "There. Are you happy?" I asked. "Now what?"

She dropped the scarf-covered object behind the driver's headrest, then extended her open palm. "Hand me your keys and your phone," she demanded. "And while you're at it, I'll need that pepper spray you put in your pocket earlier."

"What? Where are we going?"

She opened the back door and let Chewie into the back seat. I couldn't help thinking how upset Coal would be to discover another dog had been in his car. After sniffing around, Chewie sat down, resting his large head between our seats.

Florence dropped into the driver's seat. "Quit asking questions and give me what I asked for, or I swear I'll tell him to"—she dropped her voice to a whisper—"*attack.*"

I quickly dropped my keys, phone, and pepper spray into her open hand.

Without bothering to buckle up, she started the car. "I'm sorry, but you know too much." She backed out of the driveway and onto the cul-de-sac.

"I don't know anything! What are you talking about?" I considered jumping out, but, given the proximity of Chewie's strong jaws to my arm, I didn't want to run the risk of getting bitten.

Florence didn't answer my question. Instead, she picked up speed, and I realized she was heading toward my house.

"Where are we going?" I asked again.

"A place you'll doubtless recognize," she said. "After all, you saw my car parked outside it. I guess you were at the wrong place at the wrong time, Macy."

I kicked myself for letting her know I'd seen her car on that side street. Maybe I could distract her and watch for an opportunity to escape. "So...everything you said about Sterling was a lie?" I asked. "You were just trying to deflect suspicion from yourself?"

"No way." She sounded irritated. "I saw him hit Darby at least once. She broke up with him not long after. I just played up the abusive angle so the police would look into him. Darby was flying to Michigan to get away from Sterling and her nasty stepmother. Sterling had gotten worse, threatening to hunt her down until she paid off his gambling debts, although, to be fair, she'd taunted him into making overly high wagers." Her eyes sparked with simmering anger. "In case you haven't figured it out, Darby wasn't the nicest person."

She pulled up outside the abandoned house, which still had police tape blocking the front yard. Gesturing toward the ramshackle building, she said, "Guess what? This is my only inheritance from my lame family, and now it belongs to the county. It was my grandma's, but my parents didn't have the money to keep it up." She gripped the steering wheel as if trying to steady her emotions. "Years ago, I asked Darby if she'd loan me some money to fix it. She laughed in my face and said it wasn't worth a dime." With a nasty grin, she said, "But she changed her tune when she needed a place to hide after faking her death."

I pounced on the information. "So Darby *did* try to fake her own death, then? How on earth did she manage that?"

She sighed, as if my confusion were tiresome. Chewie lowered his head onto the console.

"She stumbled onto a news report of that woman who'd tried to fake her death at Grandview a couple years ago," she said. "It got her thinking about locations where she might be able to pull off a trick like that—something that would get Sterling and Nina off her back and out of her life for good. As luck would have it, she ran into Gabe Fink's mom one day, and she mentioned that her son was working in the caverns." Florence examined her short fingernails, which were painted dark purple. "You have to understand that Gabe's had a raging crush on Darby since grade school. So all she had to do was turn on the charm, promising him they could date if he'd kill the lights in the cave for a mere five minutes. She convinced him that he'd never get into trouble for it." She frowned. "I won't forget the look on his face when he found out he might've inadvertently caused her death. What she did to him was cruel."

Darby had definitely been a conniver. She seemed to have hurt everyone she came into contact with. "Was she cruel to you, too?" I guessed. "You must've helped with her scheme in the caves."

"Of course. Her plan hinged on me playing my part. The moment the lights went out, Darby grabbed the railing next to me. She cracked her phone on a rock, then tossed it and her jacket into the chasm below. She let out a scream, then climbed under the rail, where I handed her a baseball cap and a man's jacket I'd brought in my bag. She put those on, then bypassed both you and Olivia by following the railings to where the path forked backward in a shortcut to the exit.

"In the meantime, I screamed, so when the lights came on, everyone was looking at me, not at the exit area. I told you my sob story about hearing Darby's body hit the rocks, and of course your valiant—is he a boyfriend?—stepped in to save the day."

Anger welled up in me as I thought of the risks Titan and the search and rescue team had to take, first peering into the chasm, then lowering into it to search for a woman who'd never been there. But Florence didn't seem concerned with that minor inconvenience. Maybe some of Darby's cruelty had rubbed off on her.

"So she raced out of the empty gift shop while Gabe was

in the back," I said. "The woman in the parking lot assumed she was a guy when she ran past her. Then what?"

Florence gave a short laugh. "I told everyone we'd brought Darby's car that day, but I didn't mention that I'd brought my car, too. Darby hadn't planned on running into the woman in the parking lot, but she just waited in the field behind a rock until the lady went into the gift shop. Then she returned to the lot, got into my car, and drove here—to her place of refuge." She smirked.

I wondered if Matilda had noticed the car sitting in front of the abandoned house yet, but maybe she went to bed early. I wished she'd pull out some binoculars, since she'd be sure to see there were people and a dog lurking outside. It was a strange day when one found oneself hoping for a busybody to step in and act on their most paranoid impulses.

If I could keep Florence talking, maybe I could avert whatever mischief she had planned for me in the house. "So you retrieved your car and brought her food at some point that night?" I asked.

"I did. Then the next day, I brought her a late lunch before she was supposed to go to the airport. Correction: before I *took* her to the airport, like some unpaid chauffeur. You see, Darby didn't actually have friends—they were more like means to an end."

Suddenly, I understood it wasn't Olivia who resembled Becky Sharp in *Vanity Fair*, using everyone for her own purposes. It was Darby. All along, she'd been the diva in her own life, dangling people like puppets on a string. Florence, Briggs, and Nina...but Sterling must've broken the mold. She couldn't control him or his violence, so she'd resorted to faking her own death to rid herself of him.

I looked at Florence, who was watching the recognition dawn in my eyes. She gave a nod, as if verifying my dark thoughts. "She was heartless. I learned that when we were kids. If I got anything for Christmas or my birthday that I truly loved, she wanted it. It didn't matter that her parents could've afforded ten of whatever it was—she wanted *mine*. She'd relentlessly badger me until I'd accept a trade for it."

"That's awful," I said.

As if gaining strength from my sympathy, Florence kept on rolling. "Her greed extended to my boyfriends. She stole two of them in college. And you know what? Right now, I have someone I really care for, but I couldn't tell him, because she would've snapped him up like a fish on the hook." Florence shot me a desperate look. "I couldn't live that way anymore."

My phone began ringing in the car door where Florence had stashed it. She picked it up and deftly silenced it. It occurred to me that Hudson was expecting me to call him once I got home. Since I hadn't, maybe he was getting concerned.

Unfortunately, the ringing seemed to jolt Florence into recalling the task at hand, which was getting me out of the way. She reached back and grabbed Chewie's leash. "Thanks for listening, but I need to cut this therapy session short. The problem is that you know too much. So I want you to get out of the car—slowly—and walk toward the back of the house." She gave Chewie a meaningful look, and he turned toward me and gave a low growl. Dropping her voice, she said, "I don't have to tell you what might happen if you don't do what I say."

15

I glanced at Matilda's windows as I inched from my seat into a standing position. All her upstairs lights were off, and the only downstairs light was on the other side of the house. Maybe she was watching TV, but chances were, she wasn't observing the neighborhood goings-on.

Florence followed my gaze. "The old biddy's not home, if that's who you're looking for." She opened the door for Chewie and walked him up behind me, so I trudged toward the back of the house. "I saw her outside a restaurant on our way here. Trust me, I remember what the snoop looked like—I saw her interviewed on the news about how she'd single-handedly solved the mystery of where Darby Whitmore had gone."

Matilda Crump wasn't subtle, that was for sure. But she seemed to be my only hope for survival at this point, so I prayed she'd come home early.

I couldn't make out much as I moved toward the back door, only what was dimly illuminated by the interior light of the other neighboring house. Since this house backed up against a small hill, there wasn't even room for a back porch. Weeds had sprung up along the stone walkway, and discarded cups and bottles littered the area. The police hadn't bothered to cordon off this door.

Florence pulled a key from her pocket. "Unlock it and go in," she ordered.

I inserted the key, and, although my hands had started trembling violently, I was able to open the door. Even in the darkness, I could sense how close Chewie's large jowls were to my legs as I stepped inside.

"Up the stairs," Florence said, shining her phone's flashlight toward the steep staircase. Each step creaked under my weight, and the one at the very top was cracked through, so I had to climb over it. Chewie's panting intensified as he hefted up the stairs behind me.

"Go into the room on the left," Florence said.

I followed the flashlight's weak beam toward a taped-off room, which had to be where Matilda had found Darby's body. "You want me to go under it?" I asked.

"It won't matter anyway." She reached around me to yank the tape from the door.

As her light bounced around, I could tell the room was just as I'd imagined it, with a dirty mattress lying on the floor, one boarded-up window, and an empty closet that was littered with bat droppings. I was guessing Florence had gotten a little private glee out of offering Darby such a gross place to hole up in—at the very least, she could've given her clean sheets for the mattress.

She gestured to the mattress, but I balked.

"I'd rather stand," I said firmly.

She shrugged. "Your choice." She tucked her phone into

the waistband of her jeans, so the light made a circle on the floor where we stood.

I wasn't sure what her plan was, so I tried to stall her. "What did you do to Darby here?"

Florence came closer, her dark red curls perfectly framing her face. "It wasn't like I'd planned it," she said. "My only plan was to drive her to the airport, so she could start her new life in Michigan. See, she'd already set up a new identity and moved some of her money into offshore accounts. That way it wouldn't look suspicious when she died."

She took a breath, as if trying to process the events of the past few days. "I mean, I wasn't exactly crazy about the idea that she was leaving me here, alone with Olivia and the ravening wolves we hung out with. But I tried to be understanding." She tightened her lips. "But when I got here on Tuesday with her food, she started hassling me. She said the mattress was a joke, and she asked why I hadn't invited her to stay at my place. I explained that the police would be checking into me, since I'd been right next to her when she supposedly fell. But she wouldn't listen to reason. She said she'd be glad to get rid of me and this miserable town."

She relaxed her tense stance, and Chewie finally dropped into a sitting position next to her. I was tired of standing, but I wasn't about to sit down and put myself at eye-level with the dog.

She continued. "I'd brought her a water bottle and a ham sandwich, but Darby demanded a beer and a turkey sandwich. I had to go to the grocery store to get what she wanted, then go home and make the food to her specifications. The more I thought about it, the more I began to see that Darby had never *really* been my friend. It was like my blinders were taken off. I knew without a doubt that if she got in trouble for this fake death scheme, she'd take me down with her. I started thinking of what my life might look like without her...for instance, I could finally tell Briggs I cared about him."

My eyes widened, but I didn't say anything.

"Yes, I've liked him for years." Her tone was a bit dreamy. "But I'd never be able to let Darby know that. All she'd have to do is throw him one crumb of attention and he'd marry her. I was sick of hiding my feelings, sick of being her servant, sick of going along with every idea she had, just because she had the money and I didn't. Why couldn't I have a fresh life of my own, too?"

Her gaze fixed on a nail hole in the smudged-up white wall, as if she were looking into the past. "When I was in the bathroom, I happened to notice a bottle of my grandma's blood pressure medicine that had been left behind when she moved to the nursing home last year." Agitation rose in her voice, as if I were attacking her in some way, even though I hadn't budged from my spot. "Look, it just happened, okay? I thought *what if she weren't around*, and it was like my hands took over and smashed a bunch of pills and spread them into the sandwich."

She clamped her hands over her mouth. "It was all a big accident. I didn't really mean to kill her. I mean...I think she just went to sleep. That would've been easy, right? I didn't stay around to see, because Chewie started barking, and I knew he'd draw attention to the house. I planned to come back and check on her later."

She shifted her jittery legs. "Then, when I did, she was lying there, dead. For some reason, she'd pulled out this playing card Sterling had given her when they were dating —the Queen of Hearts. It was lying in the middle of her chest, like she'd positioned it there. Maybe she was trying to pin this on him in one last act of hatred, but I totally freaked out. I didn't know where to put her body, or even how to move it. I started wiping all the places I could think of that might've had my fingerprints while I thought about what to do. Finally, I decided to wait until dark Wednesday night, then roll her up in a rug and take her to the woods near the caverns, since I was sure the caverns would be closed on Thanksgiving day. Everyone would assume she'd gotten too cold after surviving her fall. I'd probably have to beat her up a little, which I didn't look forward to, but that way it would seem like she'd actually tumbled to the cave floor."

The image of Florence beating a rolled-up Darby with a crowbar sprang to mind, and I struggled to erase it.

She shifted the phone light downward. "I made a mistake, though. It was early Tuesday evening when I left, so I didn't realize I'd forgotten to shut the light off in Darby's room. By Wednesday night, old nosy pants next door saw the light and had to see what was going on. She beat me into the house and found Darby."

It would be best to try to calm Florence down, but I had no idea how. I could reassure her that Darby's death had been an accident, but that wasn't the truth. She'd made the coldblooded choice to give Darby an overdose. She must have realized she would probably kill her with it.

My phone gave a sudden ring in her pocket, startling both of us. She took it out and, without answering it, said, "What's Hudson doing calling you?"

I decided it was time to put on a bold front. "He's

checking up on me. I told him I was heading home from your house, so he knows I haven't gotten back yet. You need to let me drive you to the police, Florence. You can tell them your story, and I'm sure they'll understand." It was a total lie, but maybe she'd buy it in her distressed state.

She gave me a wild look. "You can't go home. Now you know everything. I can't let you tell anyone. It's my time to be with Briggs now." She shoved the phone into her pocket and tugged on Chewie's leash. "I need to get rid of your phone before anyone tries to track it. I'll leave you here with Chewie. He'll be right outside this door. You can't get out, so don't even try. I'd hate to have a mess when I come back."

She led Chewie from the room, pulling the rickety door shut behind them. After a few minutes, I could hear her walking down the stairs. I stood still until I heard her car pulling away, then I inched toward the door. Had she *really* left Chewie behind to guard me?

My answer came swiftly as the Rottweiler gave a warning growl. I didn't want to open that door, that was for sure.

I flipped on the light, then tiptoed toward the boarded-up window. Like Matilda had said, there was a significant crack toward the top of the plywood that let light shine into her house. But the opening wasn't big enough to crawl out of, and there were so many nails holding it to the wall that I didn't stand a chance of pulling it loose.

If only Florence hadn't noticed my pepper spray, I might have stood a fighting chance against Chewie.

I hated feeling so blindsided. All this time, I'd felt sorry for Florence. She had really seemed like she was grieving Darby's loss, and maybe, on some weird level, she was. Darby had gotten Florence into the circles where she could hang out with Briggs. She'd showed her some level of kindness, albeit attached to following her orders. In short, Darby had been a narcissist, and Florence was trying to detox from her manipulative abuse.

But she'd made it clear I presented a very dangerous hitch in her plans for a happily ever after with Briggs. It was sad—all this time, Briggs had been obsessed with Darby, and Florence had been obsessed with Briggs.

Where was Florence even taking my phone? Clearly, she hadn't thought this plan through any more than she'd plotted out Darby's murder. If I went missing, my phone's location services would surely show that I'd come to this house. The police would eventually discover Florence's parents had once owned the place. But none of this would happen in a hurry...only after Florence got rid of me.

I groaned, and Chewie responded with another growl from his side of the door. Shivering in the unheated house, I pulled my cardigan tighter. When I put my hands into the pockets, I found a half-eaten package of peanut butter crackers I'd picked up during our visit to Hinton.

Peanut butter.

Dogs loved peanut butter. When Coal had needed antibiotics for an infected spot on his ear, I'd coated the pills in peanut butter and he'd gobbled them down.

I walked toward the door, trying to ignore Chewie's ominous noises outside it. The doorknob itself was quite basic, and didn't look like it could lock. Gingerly wrapping my hand around the knob, I turned it all the way, and I could feel that the door would open if I pulled on it.

Glad to see I had some kind of out, I started breaking the crackers in two. One by one, I positioned them on the floor, making a trail that led from just inside the door to the closet.

I was about to take a huge risk, given that I had nothing to fight the dog with if he attacked. But I needed to get out of this room before Florence returned. I wasn't sure if she owned a gun, but she certainly owned kitchen knives and deadly tools like a hammer or crowbar, plus, now she had my pepper spray.

If only Matilda would notice the bedroom light and report it to the police, but it would be foolish to count on that. I had to act, and I had to act *now*.

After taking a deep breath, I gripped the knob and opened the door all the way, so that it pressed me against the wall. At least it offered me a little protection.

As I'd expected, Chewie gave a bark and came charging in.

16

Chewie's wild, deep barks were disturbing, but they stopped the moment he leaned down to sniff the peanut butter cracker in front of him. I didn't hesitate, swinging around the door as quickly as I could and pulling it shut behind me as I stepped into the hallway.

The Rottweiler went nuts, barking and banging against the closed door. Skipping the broken first step, I held onto the railing and careened down the stairs. The house was quite dark, although some of the light from the street shone in the front window.

I headed for the back door, turned the lock, and ran outside. While I could run along the sidewalks, cutting through yards and the woods to get to Bo's house, it would take some time, and Florence would definitely see me if she drove past.

I had another option, and I decided it was the best one. I ran directly to Matilda's back door and started pounding on it.

WHAT SEEMED like five minutes passed, although it was probably only one. With an exasperated cry, Matilda shouted, "Are you daft? What is going on out there?"

When she finally cracked the door open, I pushed my way past her before shoving the door closed. Flipping the lock, I said, "I'm sorry, but I'm trying to get away from Darby's killer."

She wobbled against her cane. "*What* did you just say, young lady?"

"I need to use your phone. I said there's a killer on the loose."

"Now, look here. I don't know what kind of prank this is, but barging into someone's home in the middle of the night is hardly called for."

Ignoring her rant, I asked, "Do you have a land line?" I recalled she'd said she didn't own a cell phone—or a "mobile," as she'd called it.

She gave an imperious shake of her head. "No, I don't. And may I suggest you exit the same way you came in?"

I was finished putting up with her delays. "Listen, I'm Vera's friend, and I'm thirty-eight years old. I'm hardly playing a prank. I'm serious—we need to call the police. I know you must have a phone."

The doorbell rang. Something in my gut told me exactly who was standing outside that front door, and my hunch was confirmed when a deep dog bark sounded.

"Matilda," I pressed, "The person who killed Darby Whitmore is standing on your front porch. She has a deadly dog and possibly some kind of weapon. Do not open that door, whatever you do. We have to call the police —*now*."

Matilda seemed to consider what I'd said. With the most affected of British accents, she replied, "I daresay you expect me to point you to my phone. This is some sort of newfangled swindle, I'll wager. You're probably in on it with your dog-owner chum out there."

Oh, mercy. There was literally no reasoning with this woman. The doorbell rang again, this time for an extended period.

Desperate for a phone, I raced into the living room, glancing at the side tables. I was about to run upstairs and rummage through Matilda's bedroom when a huge thump sounded on the porch. Soon after, a dog started whining.

What was this? Some kind of strange technique to get Matilda to open the door?

The older lady was making her way toward me. She lifted her cane from the ground and pointed the tip at me. "Young lady! I must demand you exit my home!"

I shot back, "What are you going to do, call the cops? I sure hope you do!"

She had nothing to say to that.

I waited for the doorbell to ring again, but it didn't. Again, the dog went into a whining frenzy on the porch, so I finally gathered up my courage and peeked out the front window.

All I could make out was the shadow of a masculine form who looked much bigger than Florence. Uncertain what was going on, I reached over and flipped light switches until the front porch light blazed to life.

And there stood my brother, looking right at me in the window. "Open up, Macy. I've got her here on the ground and the dog's leashed to the porch. Detective Hatcher's on his way."

I opened the door, staring at Florence, who was sitting on the porch floor with her wrists in zip ties. She shot me a nasty look.

"How did you find me?" I asked Bo.

He explained, "Hudson called Milo and said you weren't picking up. Milo called me, said he'd last seen you at Florence's place. He gave me her address and I headed over." He extended an open palm, and an older revolver sat on it. "It's unloaded now, but it wasn't when she got here. I watched her stuff it into her purse as she came out of her place, then I followed her here. After heading into the house next door, she brought her dog out and came straight for this front porch."

"I guessed you'd come here first." Florence sounded almost triumphant. "Though I don't know why you'd count on such an old hag to save you."

Matilda, who had been standing behind me and listening to our entire conversation, suddenly gave a dismissive snort. "Cheeky upstart."

I was fairly certain the cheekiest one in our immediate vicinity was Matilda herself, but I didn't comment. Side-stepping Florence, I gave Bo a hug. "Thank you for coming for me." I threw a glance at Chewie, who'd stayed remarkably quiet. "How did you get him to calm down?" I asked.

Bo grinned. "I had some deer jerky in my truck, so I lured him over with it, then tied his leash to the porch before Florence could turn around."

Of course my brother drove around with deer jerky in his vehicle. Made sense to me. Not to mention the zip ties he'd snapped on Florence's wrists.

I looked down at Florence as police cars swarmed up the street. "What did you do with my phone?" I demanded.

"I set it on that round table on your back porch," she said. "I figured it would look like you'd been there for awhile. Then I parked your car on the sidewalk by your place and left the key under the seat. I had to jog home to get my own car—that's why it took me so long to get back here. By the way, you must have quite the guard dog yourself. The minute I opened your gate, it started barking."

My guard dog definitely *was* something. Coal always knew who had entered the gate, just by the sound of their approach. He never barked at Bo or me, but he did at everyone else.

Detective Hatcher was walking toward us. I leaned down toward Florence. "Were you really going to shoot me?" I whispered.

She gave me a long look, her eyes full of that vulnerability that had previously spurred me to look out for her. "I really couldn't say for sure."

As the detective spoke with Bo, an animal control officer approached Chewie. Bo must've told the police there was a hostile dog on the scene. The guy managed to finagle a muzzle over Chewie's jaws.

Worry etched Florence's features. "What's going to happen to him?" she asked. "He won't know what to do without me."

Feeling a surge of pity for the beleaguered woman, I asked, "Is there anyone he likes, besides you?"

She didn't hesitate. "Briggs. Chewie is good with Briggs, and he likes her."

I placed a comforting hand on her shoulder, which

seemed surreal since she'd come here to shoot me. "I'll talk to Briggs and animal control and see what I can do."

Part of me hated to see Florence—who was first and foremost a victim of Darby's emotional abuse—hauled off into police custody. She had no true friends, save perhaps Briggs, and she didn't have any family around.

Bo must've seen the look on my face, because he walked over and stood by my side. His presence was always a comfort to me.

The detective cut Florence's zip ties before handcuffing her and walking her down the stairs. The animal control officer was about to wrangle Chewie into his van, so I jogged over and gave him my number, telling him I might have a friend who could pick the dog up and care for him. "I'll be in touch as soon as I find out," I promised.

As I headed back onto the porch, Matilda, who until now had fallen strangely silent, piped up. "I suppose I was mistaken about your intentions. What a dreadful evening."

It had certainly been a *little* more dreadful for me than for her, since I'd been in danger of getting attacked by a dog or shot by a murderer. But I managed a tight smile and said, "Thanks."

Bo gave Matilda a shrewd glance, no doubt sensing my irritation with her. I had to give her credit—unlike most women, she didn't suddenly turn flirtatious with him. She simply said, "You're her brother?"

He nodded, extending a hand. "Bo Hatfield, ma'am. Nice to meet you."

His politeness brought a tiny smile to her face, then she rapped on the floor with her cane. "Well, if you two don't mind, I'm off to bed." She hobbled into her house, clicking her door shut behind her. We could hear her turning locks inside.

When I shivered, Bo took his coat off and wrapped it around my cardigan. "You weren't dressed to be out this late," he said, walking me toward his truck. "Listen, I called Titan, and he's waiting at my place. I thought we could go back there and decompress a little with some hot chocolate or tea. Are you hungry? I can make you a grilled cheese."

It seemed like ages since I'd nibbled at the appetizers at Hudson's place. The weight of being in survival mode for hours fell on me full-force. "A grilled cheese and hot tea would hit the spot," I said, climbing into my brother's warm truck, where the world felt safe again.

17

After heading to bed with a full stomach and the contented assurance that I was cared for by my brother, my boyfriend, and my Great Dane, I slept like a log and didn't wake until ten on Saturday.

Titan's vacation time was over, and he was heading home to Virginia today. Last night, he'd mentioned that Julius would be dropping in for breakfast at his cabin, so we could meet up in the afternoon before he headed out.

Yawning ferociously and gripping my coffee mug like it was my lifeline, I let Coal out into the back garden. Immediately, he gave the half-hearted warning bark that told me Waffles must be having a little private time on the other side of the fence, even though she didn't respond with her typical retaliatory bark.

Sure enough, Vera walked over to my gate with Waffles on the leash. Her tone dubious, she said, "Hi, Macy. Matilda called me this morning, saying she'd nearly been murdered by some rogue redhead with a gun. She said you barged into her house late at night and saw the whole thing. Is that true?"

Oh, boy. Where to begin? I should've guessed Matilda would paint herself as the targeted victim in this scenario. I explained things to Vera, and she clicked her tongue. "That poor Florence," she said. "You're right to feel sorry for her. She's been shoved down by that Darby all her life." Her tone darkened, and I hardly recognized the militant look on her face. "All those narcissists will get what's coming to them, in this life or afterward." She took a deep breath. "I'm not sure if your great-aunt ever told you much about your uncle Clive. I know he died before you and Bo came to live with her."

I was all ears. Auntie A had always changed the subject when we'd brought up her dead husband. We knew she hadn't cared much for him, but we didn't know why.

She continued. "I don't think she'd mind if I told you now. She always had this thing about not speaking ill of the dead—that's why she didn't want to smear his name in front of you kids." She stepped closer to the gate, and Coal came bounding over, anxious to keep an eye on the unpredictable Waffles. Currently, the Doodle was sitting next to Vera, scratching at her ear with her back paw.

"Your uncle Clive was very controlling," she said. "Athaleen was very close to her family, but from the moment they got married, he tried to drive a wedge between them. It got to where he'd lie right to her face, then when she'd bring it up later, he'd swear he hadn't said it. They have a word for that, but I can't recall it."

"Gaslighting," I said. I'd always been somewhat grateful that although my ex was a liar, he hadn't denied his lies when he got caught in them. It was bad enough that he'd lived a lie for so long and I hadn't seen through it.

She shook a finger at me. "That's the one. Had a really good movie by that name, back in the day. Anyway, it practically drove her to paranoia. She'd ask me, 'Didn't I tell you he'd said that?' and I'd have to reassure her she had. In the end, I think she started writing down the things he told her in a little notebook to make sure she wasn't losing her mind. He'd claim he was coming home early for supper, then he wouldn't show up. He'd promise she could go out to eat with friends, then once she got all fixed up, he'd tell her she'd agreed to go out with him. That kind of thing."

"Mind games," I said. "No, she never once told us about that."

"It was traumatic for her." As Waffles stood and sniffed at the air, Coal gave a low whine.

"Quiet, boy." I took a step closer. "You want to come in for some coffee?"

"I wish I could, but I'm meeting my friend Randall at the senior center this morning." She gave Coal's head an affectionate pat. "I promise I'll share more with you someday. I just wanted you to understand that having compassion for Florence isn't a bad thing, even though she did unfortunately turn to murder to deal with her bully."

With that, Vera gave a casual wave and walked toward her house, Waffles trotting along at her side. While I'd seen the feisty side of my petite neighbor before, I was surprised at her ruthless stand against emotional abusers. It made me like her even more.

Titan pulled up in his very FBI-looking black SUV. He jumped out, and I noticed he was carrying a bouquet of yellow roses in his hand.

He extended them toward me as he approached my back yard. "Sorry they don't look super fresh," he apologized. "I picked them up on my way over, and I guess the rose selection isn't great this time of year."

I took them and breathed in their fragrance. "They're gorgeous." I wrapped a hand around his forearm and leaned into him for a kiss. "Thank you."

"I'm sorry you had to go through all that with Florence," he said. "I should've gone with you to that poker game."

I suddenly recalled that in all the craziness of the night before, it had completely slipped my mind to return Hudson's call. I'd texted Milo that I was okay, and I'd convinced Briggs to pick Chewie up from animal control, but Hudson, too, deserved an update on events.

"Come on in," I said. "I need to make a quick call first, but I'll be right there."

Titan opened the back door, and Coal followed him inside. I stood in the fall sunlight and called Hudson's number.

When he picked up, I said, "This is Macy—I have to thank you *so* much for telling Milo about me last night. You honestly saved my life." I explained what had happened, starting from the time we'd spoken on the phone.

Hudson gave a whistle. "I didn't think you were the type to flake out on me. Then, when I told Milo you hadn't called back, he figured something was up. I'm glad your brother got to you in time."

"What did you need to talk with me about?" I asked. "You said you had something to ask me?"

"I did." He cleared his throat. "I started thinking about my relationship with Darby last night, after everyone went home. I realized I've always been looking for the wrong sorts of women. It didn't matter what their personalities were like, as long as they checked the boxes I knew my parents would approve of—wealthy, polished, and from the right family. But last night, my eyes were opened to other possibilities. To a woman who's not shallow, or fake, or pretentious. So I thought I'd throw myself out there and ask if you'd like to go on a date with me sometime, Macy."

Holy moly. Hudson wasn't much older than Milo, and I was on the fast train to forty. "I'm...flattered for your invitation, but I already have a boyfriend," I said. Why hadn't Milo told Hudson I was seeing someone?

"Oh, of course. I should've guessed that you did. Hope springs eternal, I suppose. Well, my invitation to The Barons will always be open for you, and thank you for being so delightfully *you.*" He abruptly hung up.

I had to laugh. I could count on one hand the number of things Hudson and I had in common. Why he'd been so suddenly and inexplicably drawn to me was beyond understanding. One thing was certain—I could never mention this to Milo, or he'd be mortified. I could only hope Hudson would keep his resolve to steer clear of connivers like Darby in the future.

I wondered who would get the bulk of Darby's estate, now that Florence wasn't in the picture. Nina might get it by default, which was probably the exact opposite of what Darby would've wanted.

It was ironic that when Florence had decided to kill Darby for her thoughtless, grasping behavior, she hadn't guessed that in one out-of-character act of charity, Darby had made her the primary beneficiary of her will. No wonder she'd been speechless when Nina had announced she was getting Darby's estate.

Shaking my head, I headed inside to spend a few more hours with the man who truly knew and loved me. I'd take Titan over the yacht life any day.

ALSO BY HEATHER DAY GILBERT

You can now preorder Heather Day Gilbert's

next Barks & Beans Cafe cozy mystery,

ROAST DATE

Welcome to the Barks & Beans Cafe, a quaint place where folks pet shelter dogs while enjoying a cup of java...and where murder sometimes pays a visit.

After much cajoling, Macy gives in to her neighbor, Vera, and agrees to share about the Barks & Beans Cafe at her book club Christmas party. While public speaking isn't Macy's thing, she wants to brighten Vera's lonely holiday season...and she can sell a little house blend on the side.

When a lively book discussion spirals into a public roast of the mayor—who happens to be sitting in their midst—Vera attempts to restore the holiday spirit. But soon afterward the mayor shows up dead, and no amount of gingerbread cookies or eggnog can restore Vera to the club's good graces. 'Tis the season for Macy to find the murderer, or else Vera will be taking a long winter's nap in a jail cell.

Join siblings Macy and Bo Hatfield as they sniff out crimes in their hometown...with plenty of dogs along for the ride! The Barks & Beans Cafe cozy mystery series features a small town, an amateur sleuth, and no swearing or graphic scenes. Find all the books at heatherdaygilbert.com!

The Barks & Beans Cafe series in order:

Book 1: No Filter

Book 2: Iced Over

Book 3: Fair Trade

Book 4: Spilled Milk

Book 5: Trouble Brewing

Book 6: Cold Drip

Book 7: Roast Date

Be sure to sign up now for Heather's newsletter at **heatherdaygilbert.com** for updates, special deals, & giveaways!

And if you enjoyed this book, please be sure to leave a review at online book retailers and tell your friends!

Thank you!

Made in United States
Troutdale, OR
08/22/2025

33880234R00094